# Kefa's Quest

ISBN: 978-1-7343917-3-2 (Paperback)
ISBN: 978-1-7343917-1-8 (Hardcover)
ISBN: 978-1-7343917-8-7 (Ebook)

This book is a work of fiction. Names, characters, places, and incidents are either the product of the author's imagination or are used fictitiously, and any resemblance to actual persons, living or dead, business establishment, event or locales is entirely coincidental.

Printed in the United States of America.
First printing edition 2020.

Worlds Unknown Publishers
2515 E Thomas Rd,
Ste 16 -1061
Phoenix, AZ 85016-7946

www.wupubs.com

# Kefa's Quest

Muthoni wa Gichuru

Worlds Unknown Publishers

# TABLE OF CONTENTS

# CHAPTER 1

For Kefa, there was no other day like the last Friday of the month. If it was a sunny day, Kefa felt the sun's warmth warming him deep inside, especially during the morning break after his first lessons. When it rained, Kefa would lead the other boys, sliding in on the mud on their way home. Kefa would let out a long whistle as he slid as far as he could along the path, where the mud was as slick as porridge. Sometimes he fell on his bottom, smearing his uniform with mud. His mother would scold him, but Kefa washed his uniform quickly, the moment he came home. Then, he would do his homework and sit near the door, facing the gate of their *boma*. Every time he heard a bodaboda slowing down, he would go outside to check whether the motorbike was dropping off his father. Kefa's father would arrive on the last Friday of each month from Nairobi, and no matter how late it got, Kefa could not sleep before his father had arrived.

Wafula, Kefa's father, came with a present for every one of his five children and their mother. He would come wearing his multi-pocket military jacket, and upon arrival, he would remove it and place it on a table. The family would gather around him; then, he would point out the pockets. 'Pocket one, Kefa,' Kefa was the firstborn. 'Pocket two, Juma,' the second of his children. Then came Situma, Simiyu, and the last two pockets would be reserved for Kefa's mother and baby Naliaka, the only girl in the family. Each of the children would dip into the pockets, fishing out their gifts. There would be a mini celebration with some jumping up and down, others whooping with joy. Kefa's father, his head almost touching the rafters, would stand there grinning, with his large white teeth flashing in the dimness of the darkening evening.

At the end of July, the year Kefa turned twelve, his father had arrived as usual on a Friday. Kefa's father laid out his jacket and pointed out the pockets. When Kefa reached into the pocket that contained his gift, he came out and spread his empty hands, his eyes opening wide, questioning his father. His father turned away from him and continued pointing out the pockets for the rest of the family. There was a ball for Juma who loved football, and a baseball cap for Situma who took it and wore it backwards on his head. Simiyu got a storybook and immediately opened it, sitting down to read. Then Mama Angineta, Kefa's mother, removed a bright green and yellow lesso, which she tied around her midsection and twirled around with. Baby Naliaka got a baby suit, and Mama Angineta held it against her. Naliaka beamed, grabbing a handful of the soft material, and opened her mouth in a smile, showing her two new baby teeth.

*Where was my gift?* Kefa asked himself. This was supposed to be the most important year of his life.

"Dip your hand into the pocket again, son," Wafula told Kefa.

Kefa did as he was told. He searched around the pocket, wondering what kind of a present his father had brought him. Puzzled, he removed his hand, holding a small piece of paper, which he hadn't noticed before. Kefa handed it to his father.

"Read the paper," His father said.

Kefa squinted, trying to make out the words scribbled across the paper. That's when he heard *the peeepeee* of a motorbike horn behind him. His father led the family outside, and they found the motorbike rider unloading a brand-new bicycle. Kefa's father went to help, and a moment later, presented the bicycle to Kefa, who seemed to have lost the ability to close his mouth.

Kefa's father beamed proudly. "In a few weeks, you will be turning into a man, Kefa, and a man needs to have the means of getting around."

Kefa laughed out loud with sheer joy.

Kefa was to be circumcised that August. This ritual would mark the end of childhood and the onset of manhood. It was something he was eagerly looking forward to. Preparations had already begun. Several boys would be circumcised that August. There was an air of festivity in the village, and every once in a while, singing filled the air. The boys who would be circumcised could be seen moving around the village dancing, sometimes with pieces of meat hanging on their shoulders.

That morning, Kefa had gone to one of his uncles' houses on his mother's side, and come back with goat meat. As was the tradition, uncles on the mother's side were the only one who could give boys to be circumcised meat. Kefa's mother prepared it, which they enjoyed with chunks of ugali. The following day, the family headed off to the Seventh-day Adventist church near the market square. After the service, people gathered around Wafula, whom they called *Daktari*, even though he was not a doctor but just worked as a laboratory assistant in a clinic in Nairobi. The family then went to the market, and Mama Angineta, Kefa's mother, bought groceries. Wafula bought roasted flying ants, and they munched on the delicacy as they walked home.

That afternoon, Kefa and his brothers took Juma's ball out to the field to enjoy a game of football. Wafula, who had been a top player during his primary school days, got out of his church clothes and joined them in the field. He and Juma played on one side against Kefa, Situma, and Simiyu. At the end of the game, Wafula and Juma emerged the winners, having scored one goal, while Kefa, Situma, and Simiyu had not managed to score at all.

"We didn't score because Baba is like a wall at the goal post. No ball can get through him," Kefa told Juma.

"If you continue to eat as well your mother feeds you, you will be my size in a few years," Wafula said, patting Kefa on the back. "Then, you stand a chance. Maybe."

As the sun set beyond Mt. Elgon, the boys and their father left the field and were going inside when a woman came running into their homestead, screaming.

"Please help! My baby, she is dying!" She thrust the small child into Wafula's arms.

"What's wrong with her?" Wafula asked.

"*Ananyongwa*. She has something stuck in her throat."

Wafula held the child below the armpits and thumped her back sharply. A piece of meat flew out, and the child started coughing and crying.

"*Nasimu*! Thank you. You have saved my daughter," The woman told Kefa's father.

"I am going to study hard and be a doctor one day," Kefa told his father that evening.

"Dr. Kefa Wafula," His father said, "I like it, and I am going to support you until you achieve your dream."


The following day, Kefa's father stood up, about to climb on to the back of the motorbike that would take him to Kimilili town. But that's when something unusual happened.

"Baba Kefa," Kefa's mother called out to his father.

There was an unwritten rule in Kefa's household that Kefa's father was not to be called back once he had crossed the doorstep and out of the house, especially when he was about to travel. This time, Kefa's father looked at his mother with a frown on his face, one of his legs midair. However, he put a small bag he was carrying onto the motorbike seat and went back to her.

"I just wanted to remind you we have to pay for Wepukhulu's bull in two weeks' time," Mama Angineta said.

"Don't worry about the bull. Just make sure you take enough maize to the *posho* mill so that we will have enough flour," Kefa's father said, patting her hand.

The maize flour, mixed with millet flour, would be used to make *kamalwa,* a traditional brew, and it would be used by the circumciser to bless the initiates soon after circumcision.

"I will be here in two weeks with the money required to pay for the bull."

Kefa's father shared that he was going to take two weeks leave so that he would be at home for Kefa's circumcision ceremony. After the ritual, a bull would be slaughtered to celebrate the occasion. Many relatives had been invited. Some were travelling from Kitale, while others would visit from as far as Nakuru and Nairobi. It was going to be a big ceremony because Kefa was the firstborn of the family. Already, relatives had brought several chickens, while others brought maize and firewood.

Kefa and his brothers followed their father, waving at him until he had disappeared. Simiyu and Situma turned to go back to the house, but Kefa walked on. He went past their gate and down the path that went past their homestead. Kefa only turned back when he could no longer see the dust that was raised by the motorbike as it rode away. Kefa wished that two weeks would fly by quickly, so that he could see his father arriving home, once again.

Two weeks passed, and on the expected date of Wafula's arrival, Kefa's mother made his father's favorite meal- ugali and *sucha.* The black nightshade was cooked in a traditional pot and steeped in milk cream. She also slaughtered a chicken, and while she prepared it, she made sure she reserved *imondo.* The gizzard was always reserved for the head of the family.

At nine in the evening, they were still waiting for Wafula to appear. One by one, the children dozed off, and the mother put them to bed. At eleven, Kefa's mother started to doze.

"Let's go to bed. Your father must have been unable to travel today. He is sure to come tomorrow," She told Kefa, rising from her chair.

"Just a few more minutes," Kefa said, refusing to give up.

Kefa's mother went to bed, and at midnight, Kefa too went to bed, telling himself that everything would be okay. He told himself that his father would arrive the following day, safely. However, even though Kefa waited until eleven that evening  his father did not appear. Nor the next day, or the next. Kefa's big day, the day of the circumcision ceremony arrived, and there was still no trace of his father.

The circumcision day arrived, and Kefa's ceremony began early in the morning. At five o'clock, Kefa, who was the oldest, had been elected the leader, and he led the other boys towards the river. He ran slowly. Where there should have been a spring in his step, his feet dragged on to the ground. He felt an emptiness in a day that would have been the most joyous in his life. The initiates were smeared with mud all over their bodies, and as they made their way back to the homestead, Kefa prayed for his father to appear.

"Coward, you cannot face the knife," Shikada, an age mate of Kefa's father, mocked him as he escorted him to the circumciser.

Kefa hardly heard him. He scanned the crowds, hoping to see his father. He was feeling let down. He needed his father desperately at this crucial stage in his life - the transition from a boy to a man. Disappointed, Kefa faced East and gritted his teeth. *I will stand firm and not waver,* Kefa vowed, driven by a mixture of courage and anger.

After a while, Kefa's *Senge* ululated, a shout of victory, signifying that her nephew had bravely borne the knife. His mother came forward and joined in the singing and jubilation. There was pride in her eyes, but Kefa knew she was worried. Her voice cracked with sadness as she sang, even though she was trying to be happy. Uncle Sitati, Kefa's uncle, came and presented a young bull to him. Kefa touched the bull proudly, but he was wishing that it was his father would be there to witness him bringing honor to the Abamalwa clan.

# Chapter 2

The search for Kefa's father began a week later. Kefa's uncle, Sitati, a younger brother of his father, traveled to Nairobi to look for him. And for a week, Wafula's family waited with hope that Uncle Sitati would still return with good news. But when Uncle Sitati came back, the news was not good. Uncle Sitati had visited hospitals and even mortuaries. Yet, even so, Wafula's whereabouts remained a mystery. Every day, Kefa would stay at their gate, waiting, until it would start getting dark. He imagined that his father would still show up, despite everything.

Six months passed without any news of his father. The pieces of ugali that each of his siblings were given during supper time became smaller. After all, his mother now struggled to feed them. Kefa and his brothers had been sent home several times to collect the school levies that his mother was unable to pay. Then the despair Kefa felt slowly turned into anger. He began thinking his father had abandoned them. Several neighbors had disappeared in Nairobi and other big towns. Kefa started thinking that perhaps the reason his father could not be found was because he did not want to be found. Maybe, his father just became tired of taking care of them.

In the meanwhile, good-old Uncle Sitati stepped in to help them. He would visit them often, each time carrying something important: such as a *gorogoro* (two-kilo tin) of maize flour, a loaf of bread for the children, and sometimes, even a kanga for Angineta, their mother. Kefa was happy that his uncle was helping them. His mother had even started tilling other people's land to get money to buy food. Uncle Sitati would assist, too, carrying out minor repairs in the house. He even helped Kefa and his brothers prepare the shamba for the next season's planting. Kefa thought, *My family is lucky to have a caring uncle like Sitati.*

At first, Uncle Sitati treated Kefa's mother like nothing more than his favorite sister in –law. Kefa's father had planted a few acres of sugar cane, and when the time came to harvest, Uncle Sitati persuaded his mother to have their sugar cane harvested together with his. He offered to pay the harvesters and arrange for transport to the factory.

The day came when it was time to collect the money from the factory. That day, Uncle Sitati came home from Kimilili town in a taxi. Kefa and his mother were tilling the vegetable garden in front of their house, and his brothers were grazing the family's livestock outside their compound. Uncle Sitati unloaded a bale of maize flour from the boot, several kilos of sugar, cooking oil, some packets of wheat flour, rice, and to top it all, two kilograms of meat. He entered the house with all his teeth showing. Kefa and his mother helped Uncle Sitati carry the things inside the house. Then Uncle Sitati went back to the taxi and retrieved a shabby looking suitcase. Its once maroon color had faded to a dull brown, the color of old tree bark. He carried the suitcase into the house.

Kefa and his mother followed Uncle Sitati to the house and stood facing him. Uncle Sitati, still smiling, put his suitcase down and settled on Kefa's father's favorite chair.

"Why do you look so surprised?" he asked Mama Angineta. "The children need to feed, and I have enough money to feed them."

"Did you bring my share of the sugar cane money?" Mama Angineta asked him.

"I have just told you. I have enough money to take care of all of you. Why are you worried?" Uncle Sitati countered.

"I am not worried. I need to pay the school levies for the boys and buy them new uniforms," Mama Angineta replied.

Mama Angineta was right. Even though her children went to a public primary school, parents were expected to pay for levies such as activity fees, charges for teachers not employed by the government, and new uniforms. Uncle Sitati regarded her, then laughed loudly.

"Have I not been taking care of you since my brother disappeared? You are now my responsibility. I will look after you like any other member of my household."

"Wafula, Kefa's father, will come back soon," Mama Angineta said.

"It's almost a year since my beloved brother disappeared," Uncle Sitati said, "Have I not ably fitted his shoes? Tell me. Have I not proved myself?"

"When Wafula comes back, I will tell him of your generosity," Mama Angineta said.

Uncle Sitati moved slowly towards her.

"You are a beautiful woman, still young and strong. Don't wait for a man who disappeared. He is most likely to be dead. I will take care of you. I know my brother would have wanted it."

Kefa moved between his mother and his uncle.

"Leave my mother alone!" he told his uncle. "My father is not dead."

Just then, Kefa's three brothers, burst into the scene. Their mother put away the foodstuff but left the suitcase where it was. She prepared the meat and cooked ugali, which they ate. Uncle Sitati ate the meal silently, glowering at them. After the meal, Uncle Sitati took his suitcase and left.

After the incident, Uncle Sitati stopped coming to the house, and Kefa and his family began to suffer. Kefa's mother once again started tilling other people's land to be able to feed the family and buy the children clothes. Uncle Sitati did not give any of the sugar cane money to Mama Angineta. Kefa's school uniform and that of his brothers became tattered, and his mother could only patch them up because she had no money to buy new ones.

It was not just Uncle Sitati, who saw Kefa's mother as a fair game without Wafula's protection. Several men made a habit of passing by their house. Some would ask for a drink of water, and others came asking for fire to light their cigarettes, even those that Kefa knew did not smoke.

One day, Kefa was doing chores a distance away when he heard his mother screaming. Kefa rushed to her. He reached her and found her struggling with Mananja, a man from a nearby ridge. He was holding her hand and pulling her towards himself.

"Let go of my mother!" Kefa shouted at him.

"Leave the adults to play their own game, boy," Mananja said, "You don't understand the rules of the game."

Just then, Uncle Sitati came by, and Mananja let go of Kefa's mother then walked away.

"So now my brother's wife is entertaining men even before he has been declared dead," Uncle Sitati said.

"I was not entertaining him. He was trying to force himself on me," Mama Angineta said.

"That man attacked her," Kefa defended his mother.

"The clan needs to hear of this. They need to know how you are making a laughingstock of my elder brother," Uncle Sitati said.

"I did not do anything wrong. It is Mananja who should be answerable, not me," Mama Angineta said.

"All I know is, I found you in the arms of another man," Uncle Sitati said.

"Please *mulamwa,* let this matter end here. Nothing happened between us," Mama Angineta told her brother-in-law. If the matter was reported to the clan, she would be shamed and might even have been chased out of her home leaving her children behind, and they would suffer.

"It could have happened if I had not come along and yet you have rebuffed me time and again. I, who would be the rightful one to take my brother's place," Uncle Sitati said.

"Don't worry Mama, I was there, and I saw what happened," Kefa said.

"And who would believe you?" Uncle Sitati said. "You should keep quiet when your elders are talking. You may be circumcised, but you are still *omusiani,* a mere boy, and are yet to become a man."

"What do you want from me?" Mama Angineta asked.

"I want you to allow me to take care of you in every way. Just like Wafula used to do," Uncle Sitati told her.

"Let me think about it," Mama Angineta said.

"Don't take too long," Uncle Sitati said.

"He can't force you to do anything. Can he Mama?" Kefa asked.

"I don't know, son," Mama Angineta answered. "If only your father would come home."

Kefa's mother had seemed bewildered since his father's disappearance. She walked jaggedly, like someone who had been shocked out of deep sleep. That evening her shoulders dropped, and her movements were slow like she was sleepwalking. Kefa's mother did not eat any of the cassava meal she had prepared. She did not tell Kefa what was wrong with her, though he already knew. So, Kefa went to bed, worried.

Early the following day, Kefa's mother woke him at first cockcrow. She gathered him and his siblings, like a hen gathering her chicks.

"Kefa, help your brother pack a few clothes," Mama Angineta told Kefa.

"Why Mama? Where are we going?" Kefa asked his mother.

"We're leaving. We can't stay here. We have to leave. Come on, be quick." she said.

With that, Mama Angineta brought a small suitcase from her bedroom. Then, carrying Naliaka, Mama Angineta ushered Kefa and his brothers out of the door.

Dawn found them in Kimilili town, where they boarded a bus to Nairobi. They were going to look for Wafula, Kefa's father.

As the bus began to move, Kefa watched as the blue-green ridges of Mt. Elgon disappeared from view. He remembered a folk song they used to sing.

*Nishivela alee Nishivelaa alee:* It's sad, it's sad.

*Nishivela mundu khutsua ihale hange alee:* It's sad when one must go away.

*Nishivela mundu khutsie ihale shibala shilale alee;* It's sad when one must go to another place.

*Nishivela mundu khutsie ihale shibala shilale alee;* It's sad when one must go to another place.

*Oh Baba!* Kefa thought, pressing his face on the bus window, *why did you have to go away?*

# CHAPTER 3

When Kefa and his family travelled to Nairobi, they went with a woman from their village called Nasimiyu. This woman hosted them in her tiny one-room house, deep inside the Kibra slum, for two days. The five of them slept on the floor, side-by-side, with no room to turn. Nasimiyu then helped Mama Angineta get a room, and Mama Angineta used the last money she had to pay for a deposit and one month's rent. Then, guided by the other women in the slums, Kefa's mother went looking for work as *Mama fua*, cleaning people's houses and washing clothes.

Kefa's father had provided well for his family, and Kefa had never seen his mother going to till other people's land to earn money, like how the other women in the village did. It now pained Kefa to see his mother doing menial jobs just to be able to feed them. Sometimes she could not find work, and they went to sleep hungry. When things became too difficult, Kefa and his brothers moved into the streets. They would scour dustbins, looking for valuables that they would sell for few shillings. Kefa would have been in standard seven that year, with only a year to go. Then, he would have sat his end of a primary school exam. He watched pupils in their smart uniforms, going to school with heavy bags on their backs, and felt envy and longing. If only his father had not abandoned them...

It was now a year since Kefa had seen his father. He was now thirteen, so tall that people thought he was in high school. The anger he had started to feel when he was twelve had also grown. In the streets, he would get into fights frequently, and because of his strength, he managed to fight his way without getting hurt. Many of the street boys came to know of his violent temper and avoided him. Then like a pot on fire that bubbles and then boils over, things came to a head one day when he and his brothers invaded a territory controlled by a rival street boy's group.

It had rained that morning, and the streets of Nairobi were covered with water and slippery mud. Kefa and his brothers walked to Ngara to a new dumpsite on Park Road and started scavenging for bottles, plastic containers, pieces of metal, and discarded shoes. Kefa had known that this was Moija's territory, a street boy renowned for his skill with a knife. Kefa knew that the four of them would take on anyone and was therefore not worried. The pickings that morning were excellent, and Kefa and his brothers half-filled the bag they had carried. They found good glass bottles, most of them hardly chipped and even a pair of shoes with the sole still intact. The sole would fetch some money from the shoemaker. Kefa was picking the bag to carry it and go searching for a buyer when several street boys led by Moija suddenly surrounded them.

"You put the bag down and walk away. You hear me? This is my base, and I will show you war," Moija said, addressing Kefa.

Kefa, the sack still slung over his shoulder, turned and surveyed the boys surrounding them. He and his brothers were outnumbered three to one. He could sense his brothers' fear. Situma , his youngest brother, who was holding a piece of metal he had found, put it down and looked up to Kefa. Kefa put the sack down and started to lead his brothers away. The street boys parted to make way for them.

Kefa had just passed out of the circle of street boys when he saw one of them remove a loaf of bread from a small sack he was carrying. Kefa would remember that loaf of bread for a long time to come. It was a clean loaf, brown like maize stalks during the harvest month of November and wrapped in a transparent wrapper. It looked fresh as if it had just been bought from a shop. From where he was, Kefa could smell the bread, a warm, yeasty smell that filled the nostrils and made his mouth water.

Kefa and his brother had had nothing to eat since the previous night. They had spent a cold night huddled under the bridge at the Globe Cinema Roundabout covered in cartons that could not keep the biting cold away. Kefa and his brothers had woken up to a dull morning with rain falling hard. They had walked into the rain as the water in the river rose to where they had huddled. The rain had reduced, but the sun was yet to be seen, and they were still shivering in their wet clothes, with their hunger making the cold worse.

Kefa looked at the loaf of bread and thought about how life could be so unfair. Boys like him and his brothers slept in comfortable beds at home and went to school warmly clothed. They did not have to scour dustbins for left-over food or scavenge in dumpsites to get something to sell to buy their next meal. Anger arose in him, so strong; it was like he never felt anger before in his life. Anger so hot that it made him feel strong with its intensity. Kefa turned around and, in one swift moment, grabbed the sack he had put down, swung it over his shoulder and sprinted away.

The move was so sudden that Kefa was across the road before Moija and his gang could react. Moija rushed across the street and tore after Kefa, who was heading towards Kariokor Estate with his brothers in tow. When Moija reached Kefa, he grabbed the sack from behind, and Kefa swung around, and they struggled over it. Kefa fought with all his strength. It was as if his very life depended on that sack. He could not bear to let go of it. Juma, Simiyu, and Situma also joined in to help their brother, but soon Moija's gang joined in the fight, and younger boys scampered away.

People working around watched as the street boys fought, none making any effort to separate them. Some were clearly enjoying the free morning drama and were cheering them on. It was not until a police officer passing by saw the fight and rushed at the boys with a whip that the fight stopped. Everyone scattered except Kefa, who lay on the ground, unable to move. He had a massive gash on his thigh, and his blood was soaking the ground. The police officer grabbed a cloth from a secondhand clothes seller nearby and wrapped Kefa's leg to stem the flow of blood. Then the police officer flagged down a motorist and commandeered the vehicle to take Kefa to the Guru Nanak Hospital. By the time they reached the hospital, Kefa was unconscious.

It was not until later that evening that Kefa came to and found himself hooked on drips. The first person he saw was Kibois, a police officer who was known in the streets as *Mseiya*. The street people trusted him. A while back, Kefa saw *Mseiya* rescue a street boy who was about to be lynched by a mob. The street boy had snatched a packet of biscuits from a pedestrian. But Mseiya had stepped in front of him with his arms spread, shielding the young boy. The boy, about ten years old, cowered behind crying until two other police officers arrived and took him away. Mseiya made sure that boy stayed safe and wasn't hurt.

"What happened? Why am I here?" Kefa asked Mseiya.

Mseiya explained to him about the fight. "You could have died if I had not come by on time," He told Kefa.

"You should have let me," Kefa said. He was tired of life in the city of Nairobi, the constant daily struggle to survive just for another day. His brothers sometimes sniffed glue to get them through the day, but Kefa could not stand the bitter fumes.

"Why would you want to die?" Mseiya asked.

"Because it may be better than living?" Kefa posed.

Life in the streets was like hanging on the edge of a deep hole. A little shove and you would just plunge into the depths. Perhaps it would be better just to give up and fall, once and for all.

"I can help you. Some centers take in children like you and help them," Mseiya said.

"Do I look like a child to you? I stopped being a child a long time ago. I am a man now, and I can take care of myself," Kefa said. Then he turned and faced the wall, refusing to say another word.

Kefa's younger brothers came to see him the following morning, and the news they brought was grim. Moija had vowed that the moment Kefa showed his face back on the streets, then Kefa would die. Kefa knew this was no idle threat. Kefa had been in the streets long enough to know that death could happen very quickly. It might be a knife stab at the most unexpected moment or a blow to the head with a metal pipe that would leave someone sprawled where he lay. It might even be a beating by a gang from which one would not come away alive.

When Kefa left the hospital after a week, Mseiya took him to St. Martin's rehabilitation center.

Here, Kefa found several street children, some of whom he knew from the streets of Nairobi. The centre, run by a church and supported by well-wishers, had counselors who talked to the children and when Kefa talked to one of the counselors, he started feeling that his life was not really as hopeless as he had thought. Some children who had become drug addicts were treated at a dispensary at the centre and after a few days, Kefa was told to take care of two boys who were recovering. This made him think of his brothers who were still in the streets and he wished they too could join them at the center.

At St. Martin's, Kefa found out that hard work was not only expected of them, but they were expected to enjoy it. There were several workers employed to cook for children. Still, it was the responsibility of the older boys and girls to clean, till the center's vegetable gardens and look after the younger children. Many of the street children ran off after a few days. Kefa, who had been used to hard work back in the village, did not mind the work. Father Ondiek, who was in charge, was kind, and most of the workers treated the children well. There was a primary school at St. Martins, but it only went up to standard five. After two weeks, when Kefa had received counseling, Father Ondiek took Kefa to Kipande Road Primary School, and Kefa joined standard seven. Kefa would live with his mother but Father Ondiek would pay for all school levies. Kefa was so grateful that his mother would not have to worry about affording these fees.

# CHAPTER 4

The first time Kefa walked into Kipande Road, his new primary school, he walked around the classrooms, hardly believing he was there. He looked at the other boys in the green shorts, white shirts, and checkered blazers and wondered whether he too looked as smart as they did. The difficult life as a street boy was finally behind him. Over the weekends, he went searching for his brothers. He started with the smallest one, Situma and took him to St. Martins. Then he talked to Juma and Simiyu.

"Look at what Moija did to me," Kefa told them, showing the long scar on his thigh. "You could get seriously hurt or even die on the streets. I talked to Father Ondiek and he will accept you."

"They beat people in those centers," Juma said. Juma had become sullen and withdrawn. Kefa suspected he was taking bhang; a local street drug.

"They don't beat people there and there is enough to eat," Kefa said.

The two boys agreed to try the center perhaps because of the promise of food.

"During a science lesson today, we cut up fruits and looked at them through a microscope," Kefa told his mother one evening.

"What is a microscope?" his mother asked.

"It's a machine that makes things large, Mama," Kefa said. "We also went to the computer lab and typed and played games on the computer."

"I am sorry, I don't know what a computer screen is," His mother said, laughing.

Although Kefa typed clumsily on the computer and took a long time to locate a letter on the keyboard, he really enjoyed himself. He had only seen computers from afar during childhood. And he was amazed at the machine where you could hit keys and letters would appear on a screen right in front of him. It did not take long for Kefa to learn how to use the computer or how to search for information on the Internet. Kefa was also able to catch up with the other pupils on other subjects. At the end of the term, he emerged among the top ten pupils in his class.

Kefa also became involved in co-curricular activities. He enjoyed playing football and was particularly good at netball. He was appointed the Assistant Netball Captain and represented his school in the second term games.

One afternoon after classes, Kefa was at the netball pitch, dribbling a ball and practicing shooting. He had represented his school the previous week against Mugumo Primary School and had admired their shooter, who was able to score almost every shot passed to him.

Kefa would run across the field and stand a distance from the goal area, aiming the ball. Most of the time, Kefa managed to put the ball through the ring, and a few boys who were standing watching him would cheer.

"Hey, Kefa!"

Kefa turned, thinking it was someone else who had come to watch him play. Jairus, a pupil in standard six, came running onto the field towards him.

"Mr. Mwaura wants to see you," Jairus told Kefa. Kefa went with the boy, wondering what the Principal wanted. When he reached the Principal's office, he found him with two senior teachers, Mr. Mbaka and Mrs. Wachira.

"You are Kefa Nakhumwa, aren't you?" the Principal asked.

"Yes, I am," Kefa said.

"I have lost my phone, a very expensive phone. I had it before lunchtime and went out to lunch. I left it on my desk. I did not know it was missing until a few minutes ago when I wanted to make a call," The Principal said.

"I have not seen such a phone," Kefa said.

"One of the pupils saw you passing here when going back to class after lunch," Mrs. Wachira said.

"I did not enter the Principal's office," Kefa said.

"You were still outside when almost everyone was in class. I saw you. What were you doing outside?" Mr. Mbaka asked him.

"I had misplaced my meal card and was among the last pupils to eat," Kefa said.

"Young man, I know boys like you. You are acting innocent, but I strongly suspect you are the one who took my phone. Now confess and bring back the phone!" the Principal said.

"I did not take your phone," Kefa said. He felt like crying. *Why are they accusing me of something I didn't do?*

"You are a stubborn boy," the senior teacher, Mr. Mbaka, said. "Go home now, and tomorrow morning, come with your mother. We will get to the bottom of this."

While most of the pupils were driven to school by their parents or came with the school van, Kefa and his mother walked there. Mama Angineta wore a faded blue blouse that had been through too many washings and a yellow skirt that had a huge patch in front. Her feet were shorn in simple plastic slippers, exposing her dusty and cracked feet. Kefa and his mother had arrived early, and they waited outside the Principal's office. When Mr. Mwaura arrived, he did not even greet them. He kept them waiting for about thirty minutes; then, he called the senior teachers into his office, where they conversed for some time before calling in Kefa and his mother.

Mr. Mwaura did not offer them a seat, and Kefa and his mother stood near the door, the wind from outside making them shiver.

"My name is Mr. Mwaura, and I am the Principal of Kipande Road Primary School," the Principal introduced himself to Kefa's mother. "The people you see here are senior teachers of the school,

Mr. Mbaka, and Mrs. Wachira, who are also in charge of discipline in the school."

Mr. Mwaura said, "We have reliable information that Kefa is the pupil who stole my phone from my office yesterday. One of the pupils saw him wandering about, and Mr. Mbaka also saw him outside long after the other pupils had gone to class after lunch."

Kefa was later to wonder whether they would have listened to him if he had not spoken so hotly.

"That is a lie. I did not steal the phone," Kefa said.

"If you did not steal it, who did? You must have seen the person who went into the Principal's office since you were the only one nearby," Mr. Mbaka said.

"I did not see anybody go into the Principal's office. The door was closed when I was passing by, and I was not the only one. Several pupils were in front of me."

"Could any of the other pupils have gone into my office?" the Principal asked.

"I don't know," Kefa said. "I did not see anybody."

"You must have been the one who stole my phone. After all, in the streets where you come from, boys snatch phones from people all the time. You even throw human waste at people to force them to give you money," The Principal said.

Mama Angineta, Kefa's mother, turned to him. "*Apana*- My son lives with me, not in the streets."

"Mama, where do you live?" Mr. Mbaka asked Mama Angineta.

"Kibra. And my son is the leader of other boys."

Kefa had become a leader of other boys in his neighborhood of Kibra. He had organized them into groups, and they engaged in sports such as football and volleyball, and they also did cleaning around their area.

"You see, he is a gang leader in the slums. This is clearly a criminal we are dealing with here," Mr. Mbaka said.

Mr. Mwaura and Mrs. Wachira were nodding their heads, and Kefa became afraid. Kefa felt dizzy, like he was being pulled down a hole. He had had struggled for a long time to climb out of the pit of despair, but now he was back, lost inside it once again.

"I am not a gang leader, and I did not steal the Principal's phone. I don't even know how it looks like," He said through the lump of frustration and anger in his throat.

"You and your mother, go and wait outside," The Principal said.

Kefa led his mother outside, feeling like he was in the middle of a horrible nightmare. In less than five minutes, the school secretary came and handed him an expulsion letter. And then Kefa's nightmare became real. Two police officers appeared from behind the Principal's office, and Kefa was put in handcuffs and led away amid protests from his mother.

When Kefa was being taken to the police cells, he thought, *This must be what life is like. The last six months when I've been a pupil now seem like a temporary rest.*

He was charged with stealing the Principal's phone. Kefa tried to talk to the police officer, insisting that he was innocent.

"I did not steal that phone. I have never stolen anything in my life."

"*Toa viatu kijana,*" She told him to remove his shoes. "After two days in the cells, you will tell us where you took the Principal's phone, what you have ever stolen and what are thinking of stealing in the future."

"I did not steal the phone," Kefa repeated, and the police officer slapped him.

"*Unafikiri mimi ni mama yako unindanganye?*" The officer asked Kefa, "Why are you lying to me? I am not your mother! Remove your belt." Kefa did so, and then he was ushered barefoot into the filthy cell.

As he sat in the cell, Kefa finally gave up. He was now a criminal, although he had committed no crime. *Surely, I cannot sink any farther,* He told himself, resigned to his fate. *There's no rising above the muck. I'm already condemned to my life of suffering.*

When Kefa's mother came to see him the following morning, he told her, "Don't come again. I'm going to jail, and there's nothing anybody can do."

Kefa had spent the first night standing at the corner of the cell because it was packed with men, most of them drunk. Some were singing at the top of their voices, and a police officer would come from time to time to rap the door and order them, "Be quiet!" The following day, a police officer came and asked Kefa, "How old are you?"

"I'm thirteen," Kefa said.

"You liar!" the police growled and left.

At night that day, the cell was not very crowded, but Kefa could hardly sleep. As he sat there, he thought, *Ever since my father left, all of my good fortune has disappeared.* Misery seemed to have settled upon him, enveloping him and smothering him. He couldn't escape the pain and sadness, no matter how hard he tried.

Towards mid-day on the third day, Kefa dozed off due to exhaustion. Someone had to kick him to wake him up. The same police officer who had booked him into the cells was at the door calling him.

"Come on, young man, you are not going to continue enjoying free food and lodging here. The charges have been dropped against you, and you can leave."

Kefa was confused, coming from a deep sleep at first and did not understand what the officer was saying.

"What are you telling me?" He asked the officer.

"I said you are free to go unless you find it too pleasant here to leave."

Kefa could hardly believe it, even when the police officer unlocked the cell door and ushered him outside. At the front desk, he was given back his belt. The shoes he had come in with, a new pair that Father Ondiek had bought him, were missing. Kefa was given a pair of *Akala* sandals.

Sudi, a classmate of Kefa who lived near him in Kibra, told him that evening, "The Principal found his phone. He left it at a hotel in Ngara where he had gone to eat lunch, and it was brought to school by one of the waiters at the hotel."

Kefa was relieved that he had been found innocent. He reported back to school the following morning. He could now continue with his education, and hopefully, one day, he would become the doctor he had always dreamed of becoming. He walked to the standard seven class room and the standard seven class teacher, Mr. Ole Tama, told him, "Go and see the Principal before you will be allowed back into class."

So, Kefa walked down the long hall, to wait for the Principal outside his office. He waited outside until the Principal stepped outside, glaring at him.

"You, what are doing here, do you want to go back to the police cells?" the Principal asked Kefa.

"I have reported back to school, sir," Said Kefa.

"Didn't you read your expulsion letter? You were expelled from this school. You are no longer allowed in this school, and you would better leave before I call the police."

"There was a mistake; I was found innocent. Shouldn't my expulsion be revoked?" Kefa asked.

"The decision to expel you is final and cannot under any circumstances be reversed," The Principal said.

"Why?" Kefa asked.

"You are not the first one who was expelled from this school  I do not understand why you think you should be re-admitted."

"But I did not ..." Kefa started to say, then kept quiet when he saw the expression on the Principal's face. It was clear that nothing he could say would make any difference.

"This is not fair," Kefa said. "You got your phone back, and I am innocent. *Hii si poa*. This is not good."

"Stop arguing with me, young boy. I don't want the likes of you anywhere near this school. I buy side mirrors for my car every other month because the street boys snatch mine time and time again when I am approaching Kipande Road. A street boy snatched my wife's handbag, and she lost money and very important documents. If I had known you were a street boy, I would not have admitted you in the first place. Count yourself lucky because if it were up to me, you would have ended up in jail. Now get out of Kipande Road Primary School."

Kefa stayed home for a month. His mother tried unsuccessfully to get him admitted to another school. No school would agree to admit him towards the end of the year and without a transfer letter from his former school. Kefa began making *mandazi* and selling them on the streets to earn some money. One day, County Council Officers came and loaded him into their truck together with a table and all buns that he had made. After all, it was illegal to run a business without a license. Kefa managed to jump out and run away when the truck stopped to pick up more people. The following day, Kefa threw away his books and uniform, and he headed out to the streets. He decided he could take his chances there. He could survive through his wits and, if necessary, his fists.

Kefa went to the market called Sunami in Ngara, looking for work carrying traders' goods. He was hanging out on the edges of the market, hoping to catch a trader's eye. That's when his hand was grabbed from behind. Kefa turned and saw Moija accompanied by several other big street boys, and he knew he would surely be killed. He snatched his arm from Moija and ran.

It was only when Kefa stopped running to catch his breath, having run all the way to Parklands Estate, that he saw his hand bleeding and realized Moija had cut him. The cut was gauged deep, and blood was running down his arm. He tore a piece of his shirt sleeve and tied around his arm to try and stop the bleeding. It would not stop, and he removed his vest and wound it around. He hid inside a building whose construction had been halted, and when the bleeding lessened, he left his hiding place and walked to the Thika Super Highway.

Kefa stopped at the bus stop near Muthaiga Police Station. A Thika bound bus stopped a while later, and the conductor announced, *"Hamsini Thika. Thika fifty."*

Kefa got on the bus, although he only had twenty shillings. The bus sped off, and Kefa leaned back on the seat, feeling faint. The first time the bus conductor came to collect the fare, Kefa pretended to be asleep, but the next time the conductor came, he leaned down and shook Kefa roughly. Kefa fumbled in his pockets and removed the twenty shillings that he had, but the conductor refused to take it.

"Fare ni fifty not twenty bob mtu wangu," The bus conductor told him.

"I only have this," Kefa said.

"I said fifty shillings when you were boarding. You think you are clever, *sio*? I will throw you out."

"He should be thrown out," The woman seated next to Kefa said, edging away from him. "Look at his arm. He is bleeding all over the vehicle. He might be a thief."

The blood had seeped through the flimsy bandage and was steadily dripping on the floor of the vehicle.

"Heihei. Get up. Get off my vehicle right now," The conductor said then shouted to the driver, "Stop the vehicle!"

A man seated two rows from where Kefa asked, "What's the matter?"

"This boy can't pay the fare," the conductor snapped.

"I will pay for the boy's fare," The strange man offered.

"You will also pay to have my vehicle cleaned?" the conductor asked the man, pushing Kefa along the aisle.

Kefa shrugged off the conductor and jumped off the bus and started walking towards Thika. He felt light-headed, the way he had felt at one time when he had sniffed glue with his brothers. His legs were rubbery, and it took an effort to put one foot in front of the other, and he had to stop often.

It was late evening when Kefa finally arrived in Thika. He was exhausted, hungry, and weak. Kefa crawled inside a culvert and lay there.

"Who are you? Get up!" Someone was kicking Kefa. Kefa sat up, hitting his head on the roof of the culvert. He crawled slowly out of the culvert, and when he tried to stand up, his head felt as if it was filled with cotton wool, and he sat down again.

"Please, I am hurt. Police beat me," Kefa told the street boy who was standing, looking at him.

"*Wewe ni mchokoch?*" the street asked Kefa, "Are you a street boy?"

"*Ndio,*" Kefa answered, "Yes, I am a street boy."

"Why did the *ponyii* beat you?"

"Nothing. You know the police."

"Yeah. I was beaten once, and I ended up in hosi."

Kefa's newfound friend brought him a piece of bread and a packet of milk. Kefa felt some strength returning after he had eaten. Kefa stayed in the culvert for three days. His friend, who Kefa had learnt was called Rungi, would leave in the morning and come back with food in the evening.

Kefa's wound became infected. Rungi brought him some white powder-medicine to put on the wound. But by the second day, Kefa's wound was oozing pus. On the evening of the third day, Kefa was feeling so cold that Rungi covered him with all the clothes he had inside the culvert. However, sweat was pouring out of him, and his skin felt as if he was warming himself beside a bonfire. Kefa lay deep inside the culvert, feeling as if his heart had moved to his throbbing arm and was pumping out the pain. Rungi had come back with a group of friends, and they were smoking bhang. Then Kefa saw himself running from the river back in Kimilili with other boys following him. He could see his father, wearing a white coat waving at him. Kefa tried to run towards him, but his feet became so heavy that he could not lift them and dragged them on the ground. The other boys ran past him, and his father started to run with them…

"They are coming. *Ponyii!*" Rungi's shout must have roused Kefa from his dream. Kefa heard the thump-thump of heavy boots and tried to drag himself out of the culvert, but he could not move. Kefa lay there, curling into a ball, hoping the police officers would not see him. Then someone was dragging him by the legs, and Kefa screamed with pain. Kefa was taken to the police vehicle, which was packed nearby and thrown into the back, and everything turned black.

"Remove these… Now."

"I … Police…"

"Charge…Hospital."

The voices floated around Kefa in a disjointed way, and Kefa fought to open his eyes and come out of the darkness.

"This boy is unconscious, and yet you keep him handcuffed to the bed. I want the handcuffs removed right now."

Kefa tried to follow the direction of the voice and saw a hazy outline of a person in a white coat. Kefa blinked though his eyes refused to open fully.

Another voice said, "The boy got injured yesterday while stealing from a shopkeeper. He is a criminal who is going to face charges."

Kefa turned. This time he was able to see more clearly, and he saw that the person who had spoken was a police officer. Kefa closed his eyes, wanting to go back to the darkness.

The white-coated man said, "The wound on his arm is more than two days old. This boy was so sick yesterday he could not get up, let alone go stealing. I am telling you to remove the handcuffs. He is not going anywhere."

Kefa heard a click, and his hand fell on the mattress on the bed. He opened his eyes and looked around him. He was in a hospital bed, and his arm was heavily bandaged.

"I see you are awake, young man," The man with the white coat said, "I am Doctor Charo. What is your name?"

"Kefa. How did I get here?" Kefa asked.

"The police brought you here. You are lucky they found you. That wound on your arm is bad, and it has made you very sick."

"They keep saving me," Kefa said.

"Who?"

"The police. I don't know why they do it. I wish they would just leave me alone."

Kefa was in the hospital for three weeks while his arm healed slowly. Even though the handcuffs had been removed, a police officer guarded him day and night. The police officer was a young man, about nineteen years old.

"How did you end up a street boy?" Kiptum, the police officer, asked Kefa one evening when they were having supper.

Kefa did not answer. After the meal, Kiptum removed a book from his backpack and started reading. Kiptum would pause at some sections and start smiling. Sometimes, he laughed out loud.

"Which book are you reading?" Kefa asked. He was remembering how his brother Simiyu, liked to read storybooks.

Kiptum showed Kefa the title of the book, *Moses and Mildred,* written by Barbara Kimenye.

"I have read the book, it is very interesting," Kefa said.

"So, you were not always a street boy?" Kiptum asked.

"My father run off and left us. Okay?" Kefa said.

"I am sorry," Kiptum said. "I never knew my mother. My father raised me and my two sisters all by himself. I'm the last born and my mother died while she was giving birth to me. I wish I had met her. I always wonder how she looked like; how she sounded when she talked."

"I'm sorry too," Kefa said. *At least I know how my father looks and perhaps one day I will see him again*, Kefa thought.

After supper, Dr. Charo, during his ward rounds, brought Kefa a draft board. As Kefa and the police officer played the game, Kefa found himself telling Kiptum about his father, about the military-type jacket he used to wear, and the presents he would bring to the whole family when he came from Nairobi.

"Your father sounds like a very good man," Kiptum said.

"Then why did he leave us?" Kefa asked.

"I don't know Kefa. Maybe he will come back one day."

"I keep looking for him," Kefa said. "Every time I meet a man who looks like him, I stare at him until he passes. Sometimes, I tell myself that if I concentrate hard enough on his image in my mind, he will appear. Lately though, when I try to picture, him I only see a hazy outline."

"Keep looking. If he is still alive, you will find him," Kiptum said.

*Is my father still alive?* Kefa asked himself. *Should I give up my quest and accept he is dead like Uncle Sitati says?*

"I want you to do me a favor," Kefa told Kiptum, the police officer. A little earlier, Doctor Charo had told him he would be released from the hospital, soon. "I want you to call someone for me and tell him where I am," Kefa said then gave the police officer Father's Ondiek's number.

When Father Ondiek heard about Kefa's state, he came to see him at Thika District Hospital. "Your mother has been worried about you. She has come to see me several times," Father Ondiek told Kefa. "You should not have run away."

"I had to; otherwise, I would be dead now," Kefa told him.

"You should have come back to St. Martins when you got expelled from Kipande Road Primary School. I would have talked to the Principal."

"I don't think it would have helped. The moment he learnt I was a former street boy; he decided I was a dangerous criminal. He would never have given me another chance."

"Let me call your friend, Mseiya. Do you know he is a police inspector now?" Father Ondiek asked Kefa.

"No, didn't. You call him Mseiya too?" Kefa said, chuckling.

"Yes, I do. He and I have known each other for a long time, and each street child he rescues and brings them to St. Martins calls him Mseiya. I sometimes forget his real name," Father Ondiek said.

When Father Ondiek called Mseiya, the police officer who had first rescued Kefa, he came straight away to the hospital.

"You seem to love spending time in hospitals," Mseiya told Kefa.

'Moija likes to cut me up any time he sees me," Kefa said.

"You should not be in streets in the first place," Mseiya said.

"I don't want to be in the streets, but many people think street people are rubbish that should be thrown away," Kefa said.

"Not everyone, Kefa," Father Ondiek said. "See, even Officer Kiptum here was willing to help you."

Inspector Kibois, or Mseiya, as Kefa and Father Ondiek preferred to call him, called the Officer in charge of Thika Police station and was able secure Kefa's release.

Then, Kefa was released into Father Ondiek's custody.

"Never give up on yourself, Kefa, even if everyone else does," Father Ondiek told Kefa.

Then, Father Ondiek organized for Kefa to be admitted to Mugumo Primary School. Kefa had missed the end of the year exams, and he had to repeat standard seven.

# CHAPTER 5

The day Kefa reported at Mugumo Primary School, he was taken to standard seven West and given a seat near the back.

"Hei! You are blocking me!" Someone said, hitting Kefa on the shoulder with the flat side of a ruler.

Kefa turned, and there was a girl behind him, trying desperately to get a view of the blackboard. Kefa turned to face the front, and the girl immediately raised her hand.

"Yes, Zuri, what is the matter?" Mr. Muraya, the math teacher, asked her.

"The new boy should be taken to the back of the class. He is blocking us," Zuri said, tapping Kefa with her ruler.

The teacher told Kefa, "Move your chair to the back." For almost ten minutes, the math lesson was interrupted by the moving of chairs as the desks were re-arranged to make room for the new boy.

At break time, Kefa got a good look at the girl who had caused all the commotion. She looked familiar. He had seen her on the school bus that morning. She had boarded the bus around Eastleigh and had moved to the back of the bus.

Then, as he thought about recognizing Zuri, his attention was suddenly drawn away. In front of him, a strange woman was walking into the school compound. The woman looked odd, walking down the paved driveway. Kefa looked up with shock, as she was a street woman, walking in from the side he had recently left, the side where people lived, worked and slept on the streets of Nairobi– of all the people who were homeless. He found himself staring at her, wondering what she wanted in school. Other pupils from Standard seven were also staring at the woman as she approached.

The street woman wore a dirty white blouse and a tattered brown skirt. She wore a green plastic sandal on the left foot and a blue canvas shoe on the right. Her face was streaked with soot, and her hair was dirty and uncombed.

The woman walked down the driveway hesitatingly. The driveway was lined with potted flowers on both sides, and she would pluck a petal and then, in an absent-minded way, throw it away. When she came near the flag post outside the administration offices, she stopped, her eyes scanning the building in front of her. The wide two-story building was painted an off-white color, and there were two huge pillars which flanked the main entrance. On one side of the entrance, a vast mural depicted pupils in a library studying. At the bottom of the mural was the school motto, *"Learning, and then service."*

"Wait until the Principal sees her," Zuri said.

"She thinks she can just walk in to beg," Zuri's friend, Penny, said.

"He will have her out of here so fast that her uncombed hair will get combed," Zuri said and laughed.

The street woman disappeared into the administration block, and Zuri and Penny moved closer and stood nearby. Several pupils who had seen the street woman go into the administration block joined Zuri and Penny, and soon a small crowd had gathered. Kefa, too moved closer and stood at the edge.

"The Principal must be giving that woman a piece of his mind," One pupil, Maingi suggested.

"I can just imagine the look Mr. Odhiambo is giving the woman," Jimmo, another boy from standard seven, said.

"He must be giving her a look that would freeze ice," Penny said.

"A look that would freeze water, Penny, ice is already frozen," Zuri told her friend.

Kefa had seen the Principal, Mr. Odhiambo, the day Father Ondiek brought him to Mugumo Primary School to be admitted. The Principal had been smartly dressed in a light blue suit; the creases on his trousers so sharp they would have cut a fly. You could see your reflection on his shoes, which were polished to a gleaming shine.

"Remember that time, the Principal saw me spitting and ordered me to get a bucket of water to wash my spit?" Jimmo asked.

"Yeah, but you were spitting carelessly, which as Odhis puts it is *unhegenic,*" Penny said with a twang, imitating the Principal's accent.

"I spat on the dirt, and he made me clean it!" Jimmo said.

As the pupils stood waiting, the street woman came out of the administration block, but instead of the Principal, she was accompanied by the Deputy Principal, Mrs. Njoroge. The pupils started walking away. Zuri, Penny, and Jimmo stopped to listen to the woman who was talking loudly.

"They hit my child with a stone," The street woman was telling Mrs. Njoroge, gesturing with her hands. "*Mtoto*, on my back."

The pupils who had not walked far also stopped to listen. Kefa, too stopped to listen. He had heard laughter from the back of the bus that morning but had not known what was happening.

"Don't worry, mama, we will investigate and get the culprits," Mrs. Njoroge told the woman.

"What are you teaching these children? Why can't they leave us alone?" the woman asked, her arms akimbo.

"I am very sorry, Mama. I promise you. We will get to the bottom of this. Those pupils will be punished," Mrs. Njoroge said.

Later, Kefa learned that the pupils' nickname for Mrs. Njoroge was *Top Cop*. That was because she used wit and cunningness to solve cases involving pupils that other teachers had given up on. The pupils were always getting involved in mischief.

"You'd better act quickly; otherwise, we will be forced to act. Don't think we can't defend ourselves," The street woman said, shaking her fist at the pupils.

Zuri laughed out loudly, and the street woman, who had started to walk away, turned and looked straight at her.

The street woman now pointed at Zuri, and Zuri turned to flee. Unfortunately, the crowd of pupils blocked her exit, and with a few strides, the street woman was upon her. She grabbed Zuri with surprising strength for someone who looked so weak.

"She is one of them. She is always throwing stones at us," The woman said, dragging Zuri towards the Deputy Principal. Zuri struggled to free herself to no avail.

"Leave me alone, you crazy woman," Zuri protested.

"Watch your tongue, young lady," Mrs. Njoroge warned.

"You thought I would never get you, but I have got you now. You will pay for harassing us," The woman said.

"You are lying. You don't even know me," Zuri said.

"I know you. You and that dark boy with a scar on his forehead are the worst. You even hit my baby today. *Mtoto!*" the street woman said.

"I did not hit your baby," Zuri said.

"*Usidanganye.* I saw you. Wait here, you will see, right now," The street woman said.

She walked to the flag post nearby and picked a rock then moved towards Zuri. Zuri ran and hid behind Mrs. Njoroge.

"Hey, stop. Put that stone back." Mrs. Njoroge told the woman who was now circling her, trying to get to Zuri.

"Let me teach her a lesson, *Mwalimu.* Let her feel what we feel when she stones us," the street woman demanded to the Deputy Principal.

"No. That won't be necessary," Mrs. Njoroge said. "I will find a suitable punishment for her."

"You are lucky; your teacher is here. I would have shown you. You joke with people," The woman said, pointing at Zuri then walked away, still muttering to herself.

Zuri, who was still behind Mrs. Njoroge, once again stuck out her tongue at the woman's back. Kefa saw this and thought Zuri must have been the most arrogant schoolgirl he had ever met.

"Zuri Wanjiru. Right?" Mrs. Njoroge asked, Zuri. It was more of a statement than a question. "Why did you hit the woman?" she asked Zuri.

"I did not hit her. She's a liar," Zuri said.

"Those street people have really made a mess of that wall. Haven't they?" the Deputy Principal asked.

"Yes. They make our school dirty," Zuri said.

"I think they should move out of there. Don't you?" Mrs. Njoroge asked.

"Yes. They should go, far from here," Zuri said, and Kefa, listening to her, felt himself getting angry.

"I am sure you and Pato did not mean to hit the baby."

"No. I swear, we didn't," Zuri answered, and the pupils listening laughed.

The Deputy Principal sent Jimmo to call Pato, a boy who sat at the back of the classroom with Kefa.

"So, you two think it is fun throwing stones at people, huh?" Mrs. Njoroge asked.

Pato tried to protest his innocence, but it was no use.

"You will till the school's vegetable garden, Pato," Mrs. Njoroge ordered, "And as for you Zuri, go to the janitor and get a mop and a bucket of water, then clean the veranda from your  standard seven West classroom to standard eight North."

"Can I first go and remove my pullover?" Zuri asked.

"Remove your pullover? Why?" Mrs. Njoroge asked.

"She touched my arm and her hands, they were filthy," Zuri answered.

The Deputy Principal almost struck her.

"You, you..." She sputtered. "You will not only clean the whole veranda from form one to form four, but also the girls' block of toilets behind your classroom.  Then I will see how clean you will be after you are done."

*The girl deserves the punishment,* Kefa thought as he went back to the classroom. He decided then, *Zuri will never be a friend of mine.*

CHAPTER 6

The schoolboy's netball team walked into the pitch, swaggering like American NBA players. Kefa, a head taller than most of the boys, walked behind everyone else, wishing he was one of the pupils selected to play this match. He had only practiced with the team a few times, and Mr. Kioko, the coach, had asked him to accompany the team as a substitute wing attacker.

"The Nagara team is no match for the *Stinging Scorpions.*" Jimmo was saying, referring to the team's new nickname.

"Be careful, do not underestimate them," Mr. Kioko told them.

"We will beat them, Coach," Maish, a member of the team, stated.

"Correction, we will sting them," Pato, the team captain, said, dribbling the ball.

The two teams took their positions, and Maish, who was playing centre, jumped for the ball when the referee tossed it in the air. Seeing Pato wide open, Maish passed the ball to him, and Pato quickly passed the ball to Jimmo. But halfway across the court, it was snatched up by a tall Nagara player. The Mugomo Primary School team was helpless to stop the Nagara team's onslaught. Nagara team was the first to score.

Watching the team playing, Kefa could see that the Mugumo Primary School team was doing their best, but the Nagara Primary defense was like a brick wall they could not break down. At the end of the first half, Mugumo Primary School was woefully behind by more than ten points. Would they ever be able to catch up? The coach, Mr. Kioko, gathered the boys around him.

"What is happening? You guys are better than this," The coach said.

"Yes, you are!" Zuri, who was the leader of the cheering squad, said.

"The Nagara defense is pretty tough. Muchai usually gets through them, but he is unwell," Pato, the captain, said.

"You can't mean to say that the whole team depends on Muchai. You need to go into the pitch, and each of you do your bit," the coach said.

"We could unleash him," Jimmo said, nudging Pato.

"Unleash what or who?" Mr. Kioko asked.

"The new boy. He wants Kefa, the new boy to play," Pato explained.

Kefa had been itching to get to the field, and at the mention of his name, he brightened up.

"I've not seen that boy do more than shoot a couple of netballs, and you want me to play him?" the coach asked Jimmo.

"He is good Coach. Really good. He was the assistant captain at his previous school, Kipande Road Primary School. We are already behind. What do we have to lose? If anyone can turn this game around, it's him." Jimmo said.

The time was up, and the Nagara team was already getting back to the field.

"Okay then," the coach told Jimmo. "Since you have made such a case for him, you stay on the bench. He will take your part."

The coach beckoned Kefa, "Give it your all, boy. It is your chance to prove yourself."

He pushed Kefa towards the pitch.

Kefa grinned as he played. He had a wide grin with teeth, white like the snow on top of Mt. Kenya. He knew when to rush forward and when to pause and let his defenders get past him. Then, Kefa pretended to move to the left, while changing mid-step to the right. Before the Nagara team realized what was happening, Kefa was already at the goal circle. The ball curved out of his hands and unfailingly found its mark inside the ring. *I should have been part of the team from the start,* Kefa thought.

As if the rest of his team had been reborn, they played with unity and renewed strength. Within a short time, the lead by the Nagara team had been reduced considerably. The Nagara team, however, was fighting hard, and a few minutes to the game's end, one of the players managed to penetrate through the Mugumo defenders and score. A minute later, Pato, the Mugumo team captain, also scored. The Nagara team was now only one point ahead of the Mugumo team.

"We have to shoot another goal," Pato told Kefa as the ball was returned to the centre. However much they tried, Mugumo could not penetrate the wall that Nagara had built. The minutes were ticking, and two minutes stood between Nagara Primary School and a sure win. Some Mugumo pupils started leaving the field, giving up on the game.

It happened ninety seconds to the end of the game. Suddenly a hush fell onto the watching crowd, and all the chattering stopped. Kefa, who was at the centre of the pitch, had the ball, and he passed it to Pato. One moment Pato had the ball, and the next moment, he passed it back to Kefa. And Kefa, who was now just beyond the goal circle, stretched himself to his full height and sent the ball soaring in the air. It landed inside the ring, putting the Mugumo Primary School team and Nagara team neck to neck.

It was now such a close fight. Who would edge forward? When the ball was taken back to the centre, the Nagara team fought for it with all their worth. Maish managed to snatch the ball at the point just beyond the Nagara team's goal circle. Then it was a race against time. Maish passed the ball to Abdul, another teammate, who passed it to Katana, a teammate on the wings.

Katana threw the ball at Pato, but it was snatched midair by a Nagara player. Then Kefa had a chance once more. Kefa jumped for the ball and threw it to Pato, and in a few seconds, he was near the goal circle, and Pato threw the ball back at him. Kefa made the shot, and the ball hit the ring, bounced once, and then slid through. Kefa had put the Mugumo Primary School team ahead by a point. As if in agreement with fate, the clock stopped. The Mugumo Primary School pupils leapt like well-fed calves, hands in the air, whooping with joy. Zuri led the cheering squad with a song.

*Nagara boys, chokora chokora matangi*

The team echoed that indeed, the Nagara Primary boys were street urchins who ate from rubbish bins.

*Rubbish bins, eh?* Kefa thought as he disengaged himself from his teammates who were congratulating him. "Great job, Kefa!" With a few long strides, he reached the dancing cheerleaders. He took Zuri's hand roughly, stopping her mid-step.

"Stop singing that song right now," He told her.

Zuri was about to argue, but the look on Kefa's face must have stopped her. Kefa walked off, leaving her watching him with confusion.

A few days later, during an afternoon social studies lesson, Zuri had been sent out by Mrs. Mbiti for dozing in class. Then there was the unmistakable roar of bulldozers and soon, cries with women screaming and cursing. Kefa's classmates rushed to the window, craning their necks to get a better view of the bulldozers beyond the perimeter fence. Mrs. Mbiti left the class in the middle of the second lesson, knowing no one would concentrate now. It was not the first time the city council had sent bulldozers to flatten the hovels that had been built along the school's perimeter fence.

"They've had it coming for a long time," Zuri told Jimmo while going back to her desk.

"Who?" asked Jimmo.

"Those street people. They should go and look for someplace else to build their shacks," Zuri said.

Kefa, who was sitting nearby, moved towards her. "What's your problem? It's none of your business what these people have built," he said to her. Zuri faced Kefa defiantly, arms akimbo. "It's my business. This is my school, and these people have been making it dirty."

"Ai, Zuri," Jimmo asked. "How can they do that? They live outside the school walls."

"And what have they used? They have used our wall. These hovels they have built are horrible."

"So, where do you expect them to live?" Kefa asked.

"They should live like everyone else. In houses, not shacks."

"And if they cannot afford it?" Jimmo asked.

"Why can't they afford it? Isn't it because they are too lazy to work?" Zuri said.

"*Ni ngumu.* It's hard." Jimmo said.

"No, it's not hard," Penny, Zuri's friend, said. "These street people are so used to begging and do not want to do anything for themselves. They should be cleared off the city."

"Cleared off to where?" Kefa asked.

"Somewhere so far that they cannot walk back," Zuri answered.

"Maybe they should be taken to North Eastern Kenya," Penny added. By then, several pupils had gathered around, all giving their opinions.

"They should be resettled near the border with Somalia. The sun would roast them so much they would not have the strength to beg," another pupil, Muchiri said.

"Or anyone to beg from," a pupil said.

"Guys, these are human beings we are talking about," Jimmo said.

"Then they should live like human beings in houses and not in the streets. They deserve exactly what they get when these bulldozers come by and flatten those shacks," Zuri said.

Kefa could no longer hold his anger. He remembered sleeping on the street under the bridge on Thika Road in Ngara, pieces of cartons covering his body and his palm covering his face. He advanced towards Zuri. Everyone fell silent.

"Don't lose your cool, man," Jimmo said, putting himself between Kefa and Zuri. Jimmo was only five feet, and slender, so Kefa easily pushed him aside.

"Please, Kefa, don't," Jimmo told him, touching his arm.

Anger made Kefa tongue-tied so that he could not speak. He brushed Jimmo's hand aside roughly, his eyes not leaving Zuri.

Zuri's eyes opened wide in fear. She put up her hands to her face, perhaps to protect herself from a blow.  This gesture must have saved her from harm. Even through his anger, Kefa saw her fear and helplessness. Kefa had never seen his father hit his mother. He took Zuri by the shoulders.

Then looking at Zuri straight in the eyes, Kefa told her, "Your brain did not grow with the rest of your body. You need to grow up."

Then he pushed her from him so that she abruptly dropped on to a chair.

"That goes for the rest of you, you sorry lot," He added as he matched out of the classroom.

As usual, when angry, Kefa went out to the field. Finding some pupils playing football, he joined them. It took a while, but finally, his anger lessened.

Kefa went back to the classroom after the match, and as he entered the classroom, he heard Zuri saying, "That is not going to happen. He and I will never be friends. Ever. Who does that boy think he is anyway? The street people's messiah? I hate him."

Kefa entered the classroom then. Zuri looked up, and the two pupils stared angrily at each other. Kefa felt his anger rising again, but he fought for control. He took his books from his locker and walked out, remembering when the anger had started. His throat felt stiff as if something was stuck in there, and the memories came back to him...

# CHAPTER 7

The street families rebuilt their dwellings, which had been flattened by the bulldozers. One morning there was nothing, and in the afternoon, the school's outer perimeter fence was dotted with structures. After a while, Kefa heard from Jimmo that Zuri, Pato, and some other pupils had once again started stoning the street people while riding on the bus to school.

One morning, Mr. Odhiambo, the Principal, had just dismissed the pupils from the morning assembly when the street people came marching down the school's driveway. The pupils saw them, and they stopped to watch.

"Go to class!" Mr. Odhiambo shouted, and the pupils ran, but they did not get into their classrooms. They stood in the verandas to watch.

Mr. Odhiambo met the street people on the way. Several teachers followed him, and the two groups stood facing one another.

"What do you want?" he asked the street people and was answered by several voices. There were several women and men and a few boys all dressed in torn and dirty clothes. Some of the street people carried bottles of glue from which they were inhaling.

"We want the pupils."

"The pupils beat us with stones."

"We want to beat them."

"*Wataona.*"

"We must get revenge."

"Quiet!" The Principal said, and the group fell silent.

"What is this all about?" he asked.

Kefa could see he was addressing the woman who had come to the school a few weeks earlier and accused Zuri of hitting her child. The woman appeared to be the leader of the street people.

"It's your pupils *Mwalimu.* They won't leave us alone. They throw stones at us. Look at me," the woman said, touching her forehead, which had a big bump. "One of the pupils hit me with a stone this morning."

The pupils now started going closer. Kefa could see Zuri slinking behind the other pupils with her head lowered.

"Did you see the pupil who hit you?" Mrs. Njoroge, the Deputy Principal, asked.

"I cannot tell. Several pupils were throwing stones. Are we to be stoned like monkeys being driven out of *shambas*?" she asked.

"We will talk to our pupils and..." Mr. Odhiambo started to say.

"We teach them a lesson now!" one of the men from the group of street people shouted.

"You can't come here and threaten our pupils!" Mr. Odhiambo said.

"They must pay!" another man shouted.

"*Vita*! War!" one of the boys, who was sniffing glue, shouted.

"We will investigate the matter and punish the pupils who are responsible," Mrs. Njoroge told the street people.

"We want to punish them ourselves," the woman leader said.

The Principal was now getting annoyed.

"We won't allow it," he said. "If the pupils are disturbing you, then move away from the school wall."

This must have annoyed the street people, and several moved forward.

"Clear out of the school compound this minute, or I'll call the police!" the Principal said. "Go on, go!"

The crowd may have walked away in the face of his authority, had not one of the pupils chosen that moment to walk away from the group that was in the verandas. The standard eight boy was walking towards a newly built computer lab when the street people saw him.

"That one!" one of the men shouted.

"Get him," another said, and the whole group ran towards the boy.

Mr. Odhiambo and some of the teachers ran to the boy's rescue. The other pupils ran towards the street people. The melee that followed had never been seen before at Mugumo Primary School.

Pupils shouted and screamed as they fought with the street people. More street people, rushed to the school, some jumping over the perimeter wall.

By the time the police arrived, the school resembled a battlefield. Several people were injured. Penny, Zuri's friend, had twisted her ankle and could hardly walk. Both the Principal and his deputy had suffered cuts and bruises. The damage to the school property was extensive. Widows had been smashed, and some of the furniture broken. The new computer lab, which was near the scene of the fight, had suffered the most damage. All the window panes were broken. Some people had managed to get inside, and some of the computers were damaged while some were stolen. The County government once again brought their bulldozers, and the street peoples' shacks were flattened. Several street people were arrested. The Principal sent pupils home for two weeks so that repairs could be carried out in the school.

That evening, Kefa tried to read his notes but he found he could not concentrate. *Why is it that anytime I get used to school, something happens to interrupt my education?* Kefa asked himself.

"Kefa, Kefa!" Naliaka, his little sister called him, tugging at his arm, wanting to play with him.

"*Sio sasa*, not now Naliaka," Kefa said.

Just then, his mother's phone rang and Naliaka took the phone to her. Kefa once again picked his social studies notebook and started to read. "Mulamwa Sitati! Is that you?" Kefa heard his mother say and he stopped reading to listen.

"Yes, yes, we are fine," Mama Angineta said.

There was a pause then Mama Angineta spoke again, "The children are fine. Kefa and the young one, Naliaka, lives with me but the other three children are in a safe place."

"Is that Uncle Sitati?" Kefa asked his mother who nodded.

She listened for a while, while saying, mhhh, mhhh.

"The three boys are safe at St. Martins's rehabilitation centre and they have even gone back to school," Mama Angineta.

She listened for a while longer and then she hung up and told Kefa, "Your uncle sends his greetings."

*We used to be one family, living together before Baba disappeared*, Kefa thought, remembering Sikhendu Primary School in the village where he and his brothers used to go to school. He remembered how he and his friends would slide in the mud when it rained on their way from school. *Would life ever be that simple again?* Kefa asked himself.

When Mugumo Primary School re-opened, many pupils and some of the teachers sported scars. It was a permanent reminder of what had happened the day the street people had invaded the school.

Zuri, who normally joined in every discussion or argument, was quiet and thoughtful. Penny, her best friend, and the class gossiper tried to draw her out to no avail. Even when a discussion arose among some of her classmates during break time about the fight that had taken place, Zuri just listened and did not join in. Some pupils led by Kefa supported the street people, but most pupils condemned them.

"The street people should just be left alone," Kefa said, glancing at Zuri. He had seen how the students, including Zuri, threw stones towards the street people's shacks.

"The whole lot of them should have been arrested and locked up," Penny said.

"They are not fit to live with people," Nthiga, a pupil who often did not speak much, said. He had been among those who were injured during the fracas. Being very short, he had fallen, and several people had stepped on him.

"*Kwani*, are they not human beings?" Kefa asked him. The smaller boy moved away from the big boy. "And you, what do you think?" Kefa turned to Zuri, spoiling for a fight.

"Nobody should live on the street," Zuri said.

"And some people just love living in the streets. Is that it?" Jimmo asked her.

"Nobody should have to live in the street," Zuri said and walked out of the classroom, leaving everyone staring at her.

"Taratata! taratata! Here comes our hero." Penny hailed Zuri as she entered the classroom. Everyone in standard seven West  gathered around Zuri. Kefa did not go near her. He had heard all about Zuri. The previous day, she had rescued a street child at City Park when the child had been caught in a gunfight between police and a gang of thugs. All the media houses had interviewed her, and she was trending all over social media.

"I did not do anything special. I just did what I had to do," Zuri said, and despite himself, Kefa found himself getting closer to the group of pupils.

"Don't be so modest. You lined your life for that child," Penny told her.

"She put her life in the line for the child Penny. If you don't know English, just speak Swahili." Chege, a classmate, told Penny.

"If it were me, I would be busy signing autographs. You are now a celeb," another pupil said.

"No, no. I'm just …just happy the child was not hurt," Zuri said. "She was such a little girl."

Kefa could see tears glistening in Zuri's eyes, and for the first time, he realized just how pretty Zuri was. Her skin was dark brown, the color of runoff water back in the village after a torrential downpour on the red soil of Kimilili. Her nose was a little long, but with a bit of flared nostrils. Zuri was taller than all the girls in standard seven West, but she walked gracefully with her hips swinging from side to side. Zuri looked up and met Kefa's eyes, and Kefa realized he had been staring at her. He looked away quickly, and just then, the bell calling the pupils for the morning assembly trilled, and the pupils rushed out of the classroom and went to line up near the flag post.

The Principal also thought what Zuri had done was heroic. He asked Zuri to stand in front of everyone during assembly. Zuri did so, unsure of what might happen.

"This girl here acted with courage and saved a child who might have been killed," Mr. Odhiambo heaped praise on Zuri. "She brought honor to our school, and I am especially proud of her. I would like all of us to clap the special way we do for people who bring honor to our school."

Mr. Odhiambo led the pupils and teachers in clapping for Zuri, "Hep Hep!"

"Yea," the pupils and teachers responded as they gave Zuri a thunderous applause.

"How come you saved a street child? *Si* all street people trash, rubbish?" Kefa asked Zuri at break time.

"Yeah, you hate street people. What made you do it?" Jimmo asked.

"She saw the cameras and a chance for a moment of fame," Kefa said.

Zuri turned to Kefa, her eyes flashing.

"You think I am so stupid I would risk my life for fame? When I saw that child walking into the bullets flying about, I did not stop to think. I just reacted. I am not stupid, and I am not a hero either." Zuri said. Unshed tears filled her eyes, and Zuri rubbed them with the back of her hand. And as she walked to her seat and sat down, Kefa walked to his desk, too, and tried to concentrate on the book he had been reading before break time.

Later, during lunchtime, Kefa caught Zuri in the hallway, to apologize. "I am sorry. I should not have said what I said earlier; it was very unfair."

"It's ok. You and I, from the beginning we have been fighting. I should not have said some of the things I used to say. I know that now," Zuri said.

"What changed? Did you die and become reborn as a different person with the same body?" Kefa teased her.

"Nothing as dramatic happened. Remember when you said my brain did not grow with the rest of my body? Well, it has finally caught up. I am all grown up now and wise now."

"Yes. I can see that. You even have a few grey hairs in your head, a sure sign of wisdom," Kefa told her.

He was surprised at how easy it was to talk to Zuri. Most of the time, Kefa avoided talking to girls. He found he had nothing to say to them. Most of the time, girls talked about things he did not understand, and they were always giggling.

Zuri and Kefa took their food and carried it to a table at the corner of the dining room and sat down to eat. Zuri looked down on her food, spooning the mixture of maize and beans and putting them in her mouth without talking.

Kefa was curious about Zuri. Lately, she seemed to have transformed. Gone was the proud, arrogant girl, and the new Zuri was humble, kind, and considerate. *Perhaps it's just a phase.* Kefa thought, not believing that someone could change so drastically within a short time.

"There is something I have been wondering," Zuri told Kefa. "Why are you so defensive of street people? It's almost as if you are one of them."

"Perhaps I am," Kefa responded.

"For real? You don't look like a person who lives on the street," Zuri said.

"You don't know anything about me," Kefa told Zuri. "Perhaps the only thing you have ever had to worry about was whether or not your father has paid your school levies."

"Oh, you think so? Well, let me tell you something, you don't know anything about me either," Zuri told Kefa.

The two pupils finished their meal in silence, with each one lost in their own thoughts.

# CHAPTER 9

It started as a challenge. During the mid-morning break, Zuri was shivering in the cold July weather.

"Why didn't you come with the beautiful scarf I saw you with last week?" Penny, who was comfortably covered with a kikoi, asked her friend.

"I gave it away," Zuri answered, her teeth chattering.

"You gave it to who? You don't have a sister, and I am your best friend," Penny said.

"I gave it to someone who needed it."

"And me? I told you last week; I liked it. It should be mine."

"It's not always about you, you know," Zuri said.

"And why not? I am a teenager. It should be me, myself and I," Penny said.

"You have sweaters and that kikoi and others. I gave the scarf to a street child."

"What is with you and street people these days? First, you risk your life for a street child; then, you are giving out your clothes? What's your name now? Teresa?" Penny asked.

"Teresa?" Zuri asked.

"Yeah, Mother Teresa, the saint. You have become the champion of street children of Nairobi."

"Let's just say I have changed," Zuri said.

"Your transformation is like that of Saul in the bible," Penny said, lifting Zuri's arms.

"What are you doing?" Zuri asked.

"I am checking to see whether you are developing wings. You may be turning into an angel right before our eyes."

"If you had seen how that child was shivering in the cold, you would feel sorry for her."

"So, you gave her a scarf? Big deal." This was from Jimmo, who was standing nearby with Kefa.

"I just wanted to help," Zuri said.

"What have you ever done to help street children yourself? *Si,* you just throw them a few coins?" Penny asked Jimmo.

"What else can I do? I don't have money or scarves to give out," Jimmo said.

"You are serious; you want to help?" Kefa asked Zuri and Jimmo.

"Yes, I do," Zuri answered immediately.

"Me too," Jimmo said.

"Me three," Penny said, and the others laughed.

And that is how it began.

Once the challenge had been thrown, the ideas came fast. Jimmo wanted to build one big house where all the street people could live. However, when asked where they could get the money to buy the land and how they would build a house, Jimmo had no idea. Zuri suggested collecting all the street children and enrolling them in school since primary education was free. She argued that with an education, the street children would have a better chance in life

"But who would pay for their uniforms?" Jimmo asked her.

"Don't forget food," Kefa added. Kefa knew firsthand how difficult it was to think of anything else when his empty stomach growled and rumbled.

"Me, me! I know what we can do." Penny said. "We can start fish-farming at the pond in Uhuru Park. That way, the street people will have food, and the children will not go hungry anymore."

"You know when God was giving out brains, you must have heard rain and run for cover," Jimmo told Penny.

"That is not a pond but an artificial lake at Uhuru Park, which is used for recreation," Kefa told her.

"Don't bother explaining to her," Jimmo said. "She is the same girl who was asked by the Agriculture teacher to name one type of poultry, and she said hawks."

The others laughed as Penny pouted at Jimmo.

It was Zuri and Kefa who came up with the idea.

"Sweaters," they spoke the words at the same time as if they shared similar thoughts.

"Let's get the street children sweaters. At least they will protect them from this cold," Zuri said.

"We can buy *mitumba* sweaters. The secondhand ones are not very expensive," Kefa said.

"If we can raise twenty shillings from each pupil in school, we will be able to afford several second-hand sweaters," Jimmo said.

"Wooi! No pupil will part with twenty shillings," Penny said. "The pupils put fifty cents and sometimes buttons on the collection basket when we have a church service."

"And some like you even ask for change after giving fifty cents," Jimmo told her.

"So, what can we do to make the pupils contribute?" Kefa asked.

"There is one thing that can work," Zuri said. "If we were to invite one of the local Hip-Hop musicians, the pupils would pay even a hundred shillings to see him or her perform."

"That is where you come in," Kefa told her. "You were all over the internet recently when you saved that street child. Get on Face book and Twitter, and you are sure to get a response."

The pupils went to Mrs. Njoroge, the Deputy Principal, with the idea, and she was very enthusiastic and promised her full support. The idea of giving a sweater to 'a street child' was going to work. Kefa thought.

The most popular band, the *Ghetto Band,* which had the most trending song in all of Kenya, then came to Mugumo Primary School to perform the following week. As Zuri had said, almost every one of the more than five hundred pupils paid the entrance fee of one hundred shillings into the hall where the band would play. The teachers and other adults were paying two hundred shillings. Zuri and her group were able to raise almost ten thousand shillings. The following day on Saturday, Zuri and Penny went to Gikomba open-air market and bought second-hand sweaters. Then the four of them Zuri, Penny, and Kefa and Jimmo started by distributing the sweaters to the street children around the city centre.

Kefa, who knew many of the children in the city centre, gathered some of the children at the Kencom bus stop on City hall Way. The street children made a queue and the four friends gave each child a sweater.

"You were here before; I have seen you. Go away!" Penny told a boy who was her age who was coming for a second sweater.

"Hey, give me a sweater. *Umeniona?*" The boy, who was holding a bottle of glue in one hand said, snatching a sweater from Penny.

"Give back the sweater Vinnie, I saw you in the line earlier," Kefa told the boy. "If you take two sweaters, some of your friends may not get any."

"Haiya! You know me!" The boy said.

"I think I know, you too. Are you not…?" The boy seemed to lose track of his thoughts and he walked away, looking over his shoulder at Kefa.

Many of the children put on their sweaters and they stood admiring each other, smiling and laughing.

Zuri and Penny dressed the youngest children.

The day the four friends went to distribute sweaters at the city park, it got quite late in the day, and they still had more sweaters.

"Wait here," Zuri said and took all the remaining sweaters. She ran off and disappeared around a bush. When she came back, she was empty-handed.

"Where are the sweaters?" Kefa asked her.

"Oh, I gave them to a friend I know who will distribute them," she said.

"Who?" Jimmo asked.

"I would rather not say," Zuri said.

The idea of sweaters for street children spread around schools in Nairobi, and soon many schools were involved in raising funds to buy sweaters.

# CHAPTER 10

Kefa was in a curtained-off part of their room studying when there was a knock at the door. Mama Angineta, his mother, answered the door, Kefa heard the voice of Nasimiyu, the woman who had hosted them when they first came to Nairobi. He had known Nasimiyu had travelled to the village, and he was wondering why she showed up at their house so late.

"There is going to be a burial in the village," Nasimiyu said even before she had taken a seat.

"A burial, whose burial?" Angineta asked.

"Funeral rights are going to be performed for your husband two weeks from now," Nasimiyu responded.

"*Ati?* Wafula is not dead."

"Well, the story in the village is, someone told Sitati, your brother-in-law, that Wafula was found dead and was buried as an unclaimed body," Nasimiyu said.

"They lie. Wafula is not dead. I'd know it if he was."

"I went to Sitati myself and asked him, and he said *sio* story. It's the truth. Said that a friend of his who works at the city mortuary told him."

"He lies. Only two years since Wafula disappeared, and he already wants to declare him dead. He wants Wafula's land."

"I agree, it's too soon to give up hope, but Sitati has convinced the whole of *Abamalwa* clan. You know he was always greedy. He wants what his brother owned, and he is doing everything to get it," Nasimiyu said.

"I won't agree. I'll travel to the village and stop this. I will fight him," Mama Angineta said.

"You may not be welcome in the village. Sitati, he says you know what killed Wafula. Says that is why you ran away."

"What? Me!" Mama Angineta asked. "I pray for Wafula's return every day. How can Sitati say I killed him?"

"Ha, I told you. Sitati has always wanted what his brother has. Everything. Remember, he said you would suffer?"

"I'll not let him take my children's inheritance. Kefa and Juma are now young men, and Situma and Simiyu are not too young. We will fight for what is ours. The clan will have to consider my children. They are Wafula's children," Mama Angineta said.

"Sitati is ahead of you on that. He told the clan you gave away all your children. He said you sold them."

"*Nani?* Me?" Mama Angineta asked, "I sold my children? Who told him that?"

"He said you told him."

Kefa came out from behind the curtain to listen better. "Your uncle wants your father's land," Kefa's mother told him. "That is why he is in such a hurry to have your father's burial rites performed."

"I will stop him, Mama. I will not allow him to take our inheritance," Kefa said.

Kefa was angry at his uncle but more so towards his own father. *What kind of a man abandons his family to fend for themselves, even to the threat of losing their inheritance?* Kefa wondered. He vowed, *I will not let Uncle Sitati rob family of the only thing we own in the world, our land. I'm the man in my family now— I am only a few weeks shy of my fifteenth birthday. But I feel much older than my years. Harsh experiences have matured me. I will fight for what rightfully belongs to my family.*

Kefa travelled to Kimilili the following day. He arrived late in the afternoon and went to his family's house. He was surprised to find a woman there with two young children.

"Who are you?" Kefa asked.

The woman said, "Go and ask Uncle Sitati."

Kefa knew where he could find his uncle. Uncle Sitati spent his days at *busaa*, traditional liquor dens. Sure enough, Kefa found him in one of them. Sitati was with a group of men, and they sat around a huge guard drinking from it using straws. Kefa shook hands all round. Sitati, his uncle, invited Kefa, "Join us."

"No thanks," Kefa said.

"I think Wafula's son wants to have a word with you," one of the men said, and Uncle Sitati rose although reluctantly. Kefa and Uncle Sitati walked a distance away together.

"Who is that living in our house?" Kefa asked.

"Oh, you two have not met before? That is your aunt. She is my youngest wife," Uncle Sitati said.

"Why is she in our house, then?" Kefa asked.

"Young boy, I don't have to answer to you. Your mother abandoned that homestead. No one chased her from here."

"My father built that house for us," Kefa said.

"Your mother should be living in that house, but she thinks living in the slums in Nairobi is better," Uncle Sitati said.

Kefa looked at his uncle, wanting to strike him. Kefa's mother worked every day of the week without rest. She moved from house to house, washing people's clothes, cleaning their homes, cooking for them. She would have preferred to stay in the village were it not for this man who was now standing there insulting her. Kefa fought to control the urge to hit his uncle. He knew it would be a taboo to do so, and he jammed his fisted hands into his pocket.

"My mother was told that you are planning to hold funeral rights for my father," Kefa told his uncle.

"Are you here to attend the ceremony? Well, you are certainly welcome. As a matter of fact, it's important that you be here as Wafula's firstborn. But tell me, what about your adopted parents? Are they okay with you being here?" Uncle Sitati asked.

"I have not been adopted, and neither has any of my siblings, and my father is not dead. You cannot hold funeral rites for him."

"Young man, a young bull doesn't swagger in the pen before it is ready for the wrestling field. Who are you to tell the clan what it can or not do?" Uncle Sitati asked him.

"You have lied to the clan," Kefa told his uncle.

"Be careful, young man. This is not the city where you don't respect your elders," Uncle Sitati told him.

"You cannot take our inheritance. My father owns the land on which our house is built. It's our birthright," Kefa said.

"You are right. I will not take away your inheritance. But that land where your father built a house is now rightfully mine. After all, I am the oldest living son of Wanyonyi. Your inheritance is now that piece of land beyond where we plant sugar cane. If your mother gets tired of roaming the city, she can come home, and the clan will build a house for her," Uncle Sitati said.

The land Kefa's uncle was referring to was rocky, and nothing grew there. Uncle Sitati had taken the prime piece of land Kefa's father had been given by his grandfather. Kefa decided he would appeal to his grandfather. Maybe the old man would stop Uncle Sitati's plans to disinherit Wafula's family. Uncle Sitati's mocking laughter followed him as he walked away.

Wanyonyi, Kefa's grandfather, was known as *Enjofu*, the elephant, by his age mates. Kefa's father had told him that as a young man, Wanyonyi's strength had been the talk of all the surrounding villages. In a few minutes, he could fell a tree, which could take two average men an hour. It was said he was the direct descendant of Mango, a legendary Bukusu hero who, according to legend, had slain a serpent that was notorious for killing Bukusu herders and their livestock. It was said that Mango had been begged by his mother and his tribesmen not to try killing the snake, but he was a courageous man. According to the legend, Mango had smeared his body with clay to mask his body odor, armed himself with a sword, and crept into the snake's cave. In the evening, the serpent arrived. It first went around the cave to ascertain its safety before entering it. And was normal, the snake turned around and put its head at the mouth of the cave. Meanwhile, the rest of the body remained inside the cave. Mango had cleverly placed a log at the entrance of the cave, so when the snake rested its head on it, Mango chopped the snake's head off, earning the respect and love of his community.

A similar story of heroism was told about Wanyonyi, Kefa's grandfather. The story that was told was that at one time, a young bull went crazy and was chasing people around the village. A runner was sent to call Wanyonyi, who had travelled to a nearby village. On arrival, Wanyonyi had fearlessly approached the young bull, which was snorting and pawing the ground. The bull had come at him head down, deadly horns at the ready. Wanyonyi had sidestepped the beast when it was a few inches away then grabbed its neck. Man, and animal had wrestled.

The bull stamped its hooves and tried to twist out of Wanyonyi's hold, but he had held on with almost superhuman strength. This battle had gone on for a long time while the gathered crowd urged Wanyonyi on. Finally, the animal recognized Wanyonyi's superior strength and calmed down. Wanyonyi had put a rope around its neck and led it to the owner. The story had become part of the folklore of the village.

Now the legendary Enjofu was weak. Since his wife had died, Kefa's mother had been taking care of him, but it seemed since Kefa's family had left the village, the old man had no one to take care of him. He had grown very thin, and he now looked like the scarecrows that Kefa and his brothers used to erect in their shamba to scare away birds. It was apparent that Uncle Sitati, Kefa's uncle, had neglected the old man. Kefa, almost in tears, cooked for the old man and cleaned him. The old man was so far gone; he was incoherent. He kept confusing Kefa with his father. Kefa knew he would not get any help from him.

Kefa tried to appeal to the clan, but Uncle Sitati was there, countering everything he tried to say. When Kefa said his father was not dead, Uncle Sitati asked him whether he had ever seen him anywhere in Nairobi.

"You know, son," Wesonga, the senior-most elder, advised Kefa. "If you are so worried about losing your inheritance, then ask your mother to come home and take her rightful place among Sitati's wives."

Kefa almost shuddered to think of his mother as Sitati's wife. It would only be a life of misery. His uncle would acquire another pair of hands to work for him. Kefa used to see his uncle wearing a different suit every Sunday. Meanwhile, even though Uncle Sitati's wives worked to make the money to buy the suits, they would only get one new dress per year. Uncle Sitati would even take food money to go and drink and then demand for food when he came back from drinking.

Frustrated, Kefa begged the clan, "Please. Allow for more time before the burial rites are performed."

The senior-most elder of the Abamwala clan gave the final word, "We will wait for one month and no more. Then, we will hold the ceremony."

# CHAPTER 11

Kefa returned to Nairobi, feeling as if a huge weight was smashing down on his head, pressing him downwards. Kefa knew that his family was facing two difficult choices. If his mother returned home and married Uncle Sitati, then it would mean that Kefa and his siblings would have to drop out of school. After all, none of Uncle Sitati's children had gone beyond Primary School. If one of his sons were about to complete primary school, Uncle Sitati would brag, "I'm about to get another worker for the sugar cane farm!" For his daughters, a marriage deal would be sealed by the second term of the final year. They would be married off to old men. *I can't let the same fate befall my sister Naliaka,* Kefa vowed, his mind going around in circles, nowhere near getting an answer to his family's predicament.

The end of term exams was drawing closer, but Kefa could hardly concentrate on his studies. The time when his father would be declared dead by the clan was also drawing closer every day that passed, and then his family's fate would be sealed. His family had resumed the search for his father, Wafula, but so far, their efforts were fruitless. Kefa was beginning to think his uncle Sitati may have been right. Juma had moved from St. Martin's rehabilitation centre to Kibra so that he and Kefa would search for their father. Juma would search during the day while Kefa would walk around the streets of Nairobi estates every evening after school. Over the weekends, the two boys took their search to the outlying towns of Ruiru, Rongai, and Kangemi.

One day, Kefa's mother was told by someone that a man fitting his father's description had a stall at the main Thika bus stage where he worked, mending shoes. Kefa's mother had given him all the money she had earned cleaning somebody's house the previous day. Kefa had set out early morning on a Saturday and made his way where he had been directed. From a distance, Kefa saw a big dark man bent over a shoe, and hope made him quicken his step. Then the man had stood up just as Kefa was approaching, and disappointment choked Kefa. He stood there, staring at the man. The man was shorter than his father, and his front teeth protruded, making him appear as if he was biting his lower lip. That evening Kefa's family slept hungry. Naliaka cried throughout the night, asking for food, and Kefa lay awake, angry, and despondent.

Kefa withdrew from his friends Zuri, Jimmo and Penny. The four pupils had developed a friendship when they launched the *'One sweater for a Street child campaign.'* His friends could not understand what assailed him, and he was not forthcoming.

He became closed in on himself, silent and miserable. Kefa's anger, which had always simmered below the surface, threatened to consume him. Although he was a head taller than his uncle, Uncle Sitati had made him feel like a little boy. *My father told me I was turning into a man*, Kefa remembered. *Then why did he have to abandon me at the onset of manhood and leave me with his responsibilities?*

A week before exams began, Kefa, Jimmo, Penny, and Zuri were called into the Deputy Principal's office. Now, a summons from Mrs. Njoroge, whom the pupils had nicknamed 'Top Cop,' would typically have a pupil in a nervous state. The discipline mistress's punishments were feared.

Once, Penny had left class a few minutes early to buy a snack at the school canteen. Unfortunately for her, Mrs. Njoroge had seen her, and she was made to eat a whole loaf of bread in one sitting. The Deputy Principal had once overheard Jimmo, Kefa, and a few other boys speaking 'Sheng' the slang language spoken informally that was expressly banned from the school. The boys were made to walk around a whole week with signs on their backs in large block letters reading, 'I AM A FOOL, I SPEAK SHENG.'

As the four pupils waited to be ushered into her office, Kefa was thinking about the previous week. He had come to school late on Thursday and Friday because he had had to take his sister Naliaka to a daycare centre. His mother had reported for *Kibarua* – casual work, very early those two days.

However, when the four pupils were ushered into the deputy's office, Kefa was surprised to find a cheerful Mrs. Njoroge, her normally stern face lit up with a smile. She was seated with a smartly dressed lady in a navy-blue skirt and white blouse and a gentleman who was dressed in a charcoal grey suit.

"This is Ms. Nyaboke Oloo and Mr. Asaad Ghedi," Mrs. Njoroge began the introductions. "They are from 'Okoa Watoto,' a non-governmental organization that is involved in the rehabilitation of street children."

"We heard about the 'One sweater for a street child' campaign that you pupils started." Ms. Nyaboke said.

"Your initiative is very impressive, and our organization has decided to honor you for your efforts," Mr. Asaad said.

"You are hereby invited to attend a diner at Serena Hotel on Saturday, which will be hosted in honor of all who have made contributions in lessening the suffering of street children," Ms. Nyaboke told Kefa and his friends. The four pupils looked at one another, smiling.

"We are going to be on TV? I don't have anything to wear," Penny said, rising to her feet.

"We have invited all the media houses. So yes, you are going to be on TV," Ms. Nyaboke said, smiling.

"And you don't have to worry about what you are going to wear; you are going to be in your school uniform," said Mrs. Njoroge.

"You have to walk in here with a swagger as if this is a place you frequently visit," Penny said on Saturday evening, gliding through the lobby of Serena Hotel.

Kefa, Zuri, Penny, and Jimmo had been driven to the hotel by the Principal, Mr. Odhiambo, and the Deputy Principal, Mrs. Njoroge. Jimmo had come with his father and mother, and so had Penny. Zuri had come with her mother. Kefa would have liked his mother to be there, but there was no one to look after his little sister Naliaka in the evening, and Kefa had come alone.

The group was led towards their reserved table. The tables were covered with beautiful checked cloth, and the big chandeliers cast a glow, making the cutlery on the table spackle and making the ambiance seem magical.


"We will watch Odhis and follow what he is doing," Penny, who seemed confused by the cutlery on the table, whispered to Zuri.

"I thought you come here often?" Zuri asked her friend.

Ever since they had been told they would come to diner at Serena, Penny had been boasting about having gone to the place several times. Penny looked away and said nothing.

The dinner was delicious, although the pupils could not name half of what they ate. Kefa wished his brothers and sister were there. The food that was served to them that night would have fed his family for a week.

After the meal, the master of the ceremony started calling out the groups of people who were being feted. As Zuri's name was called, she walked on to the podium proudly, followed by Kefa and the two other pupils. Zuri's eyes sought out her mother as she was accepting the award. She proudly waved the trophy, which was inscribed, '*For service to mankind.*' Then, from the crowd, Kefa saw a man wave at Zuri, and her smile widened. Kefa could see the man was strongly built, seeming to take a lot of space around him, and he dwarfed everyone nearby. Kefa craned his neck to see this strange man better. However, the man had a hat pulled low over his face, and he kept his head lowered. *Could it be Zuri's father?* Kefa asked himself, but then a journalist thrust a microphone at him, and Kefa turned to answer a question. After the ceremony, Kefa looked for the man who had waved at Zuri, and he could see Zuri too scanning the crowd of people. The man seemed to have disappeared.

"You should have been there." Jimmo was telling Chege, their classmate, the following Monday. "There was so much food; we were served three times."

"It is called a three-course meal you *fala*," Penny told him.

"Don't call me a fool. How do you know it's called a three-course meal miss know it all?" Jimmo asked her.

"Well..." Penny hedged.

"She heard it from Odhis. He was telling Mrs. Njoroge, *'Thet was a splendid three-course meal.'*" Zuri told Jimmo. Kefa tried to smile, and he ended up pursing his lips instead.

"What is bothering you, Kefa?" It was Zuri who asked the question. "Ever since you came back from the village, you look as if you have been told the world is collapsing, and you are the only one who can hold it up."

"He must be having a problem," Penny said with a frown on her chubby face. "He looks as if he has been told to run three laps around the football field."

"Speak for yourself, Penny," Jimmo said. "Some of us like putting one foot in front of the other. Not just when rushing to the dining hall or the school canteen."

It was Jimmo in whom Kefa told his problems. He told him about his father's disappearance and the family's desperate search that had now turned frantic. Jimmo suggested they enlist the help of Zuri and Penny, and Kefa, feeling desperate, reluctantly agreed. Kefa could hardly wait for the afternoon to end, and he immediately left to continue searching.

The following day, it was not until it was almost dark when Kefa arrived at home with his shoulders stooped as if he indeed carried all the troubles of the world on his shoulders, as Zuri had said. Kefa had almost given up on the search for his father. He had walked around Nairobi until the heels of the only pair of shoes he owned were bent, and the soles worn out. That morning, someone had directed him to Kangemi, where a man who resembled his father worked as a watchman. Kefa's hopes had been raised, and he had walked from Kibra to Kangemi only to be disappointed to find the watchman was not his father.

His brother Juma had already given up. The previous night Kefa had quarreled with him when Juma had said, "I cannot continue with the fruitless search for a man who is most likely dead." Kefa had lashed out at his brother at those words. His mind could not accept that his father could be dead. Although he felt angry towards his father, Kefa still longed for the man who had raised him as a child. The man who had taken care of him, protected and guided him.

Kefa pushed the curtain, screening the door to their house, but he did not get in. He paused with one foot in and one foot out. It was if he was playing a game they used to play called *Statue*. In this game, when your friend said "Statue!" you were supposed to freeze and stay in the same position until your playmate shouted, "Off!"

"Kefa is here!" Juma, who was seated near the door, said.

Kefa entered the house, his mouth still slightly open. His friends Jimmo, Penny, and Zuri were in his house, sitting on stools around a table, drinking tea, and eating mandazi.

"Hello, Kefa."

Kefa turned, and it took a moment to recognize Mr. Odhiambo, who was sitting cross-legged on a sack on the floor, playing with Naliaka, his little sister. The Mugumo Primary School Principal was dressed in a pair of faded jeans, a loose t-shirt, open sandals and a baseball cap worn backward on his head, the way Juma usually wore his.

"I am sorry, Mr. Odhiambo I did not come to school today," Kefa said, thinking that was why the Principal and his classmates were there.

"That's ok, Kefa. That is not why we are here. Zuri has something to tell you," Mr. Odhiambo told him.

"I know where your father lives, Kefa," Zuri said. "I met a man who saved me from thugs once at City Park. I have described him to your mother."

Mama Angineta told Kefa, "His name is Wafula, just like your father."

"He lives in a shack at the park. I don't know why I did not see the resemblance," Zuri said.

"No. It can't be him." Kefa said, refusing to hope again, "My brothers and I lived in the streets for almost a year. How come we never met him?"

"I don't know. The man looks so much like you. It has to be him."

"I don't believe you. Why are you making up such a story, Zuri?" Kefa asked.

"I am not making up a story. Why would I do that?"

"Because you hate me."

"Zuri doesn't hate you, Kefa, and I am sure she is not making up a story," Jimmo told his friend.

"Yes, she does. She hates street people. She thinks we are rubbish," Kefa said.

"I did not even know you had lived in the streets until now, and I don't hate street people. The man I am talking about is a street person. He saved my life." Zuri told Kefa.

Zuri told Kefa how she had met the man she believed was Wafula, Kefa's father.

"Remember that time street people came and attacked us in school? Zuri asked.

"Yes, I remember, and it was because you and some other pupils used to throw stones at them," Kefa said.

"I stopped that," Zuri said then continued, "When we were told to stay home for two weeks, I got bored after a week and started going to the school library to read. One day, the book I was reading became very interesting and I forgot about the time. It was only when Maria, the school librarian, told me she was closing the library that I left to go home. It was past five o'clock in the evening. I did not have money to pay for a *matatu* from Parklands where our school is to Eastleigh, and I took a shortcut through City Park. I was in the middle of the park when I looked behind and in front of me, and I realized that I was... Was alone."

Kefa could see Zuri shivering at the memory. He knew City Park well, and he remembered how, in some places, the bushes were very thick, and trees grew close together.

"The sun was setting, and it was getting dark quickly inside the park because of the trees," Zuri continued. "I could hear the cars on Prof. Wangari Maathai Road and hurried on, running to get to the road. I did not make it to the road. My foot caught on a protruding root, and I fell to the ground."

"You should have got up and continued running," Penny said. "If I were you, hai! I would have run faster than Eliud Kipchoge, the marathon champion."

"I could not run Penny, my foot was twisted, and it was painful even to get up from the ground," Zuri said.

"What happened?" Kefa asked.

Zuri closed her eyes for a moment, then took a deep breath and continued, "I tried to get up, placing my palm on the ground, but then I heard footsteps, and when I looked up, I was surrounded by six men. They wore long black coats, and because it had suddenly turned darker, I could not see their faces. One of the men picked me up, and the pain from my twisted foot made me cry out. Then…then… they started tearing my clothes."

Zuri was now shaking so hard she was rattling the chair she was sitting on. She put her face in her hands, and Kefa could see tears flowing down her fingers.

"*Walikuumiza?*" Kefa's mother asked Zuri, "Did the thugs hurt you?"

Zuri removed her hands from her face and looked up, a tremulous smile playing on her lips.

"Someone appeared suddenly from the bushes, a man who stood a head taller than all the thugs and he beat at them and picked me, then he moved with me deep inside the park. I thought I was going to be killed for sure."

"Then you escaped. *Sio?* You ran off, and the man could not catch you?" Penny said.

"Are the one telling the story, Penny?" Jimmo asked her.

"Sorry, but Zuri is here, so she did not die," Penny said.

"Shut up, Penny," Kefa and Jimmo said together.

"Penny is half right," Zuri said. "I did try to escape when the man had taken me into his shack and was lighting a candle. I tried to creep outside, but it was like the man had eyes at the back of his head," Zuri said.

"Like Mrs. Njoroge, the Deputy Principal," Penny said.

"The Deputy Principal has eyes at the back of her head?" Mr. Odhiambo asked.

"No, no," Penny said, giggling. "It's just that she always knows when someone is doing something wrong even when her back is turned."

"I could not get away," Zuri said. "The man grabbed me and pulled me back. I tried to beg him to let me go back; he ignored me. And then he did something."

"What did he do?" Jimmo asked.

Everyone was now leaning towards Zuri.

"The man reached inside a wooden box that was in one corner of the hovel, he removed a white coat and threw it at me, telling me to cover myself."

"A…a white coat?" Kefa asked.

There was a quiver in his voice.

"Yes, as white as the whiteboards in the computer lab at school," Zuri said. "Then the man…he… he took my foot in his hands and felt the swelling, and he told me the foot was sprained, but it was not broken. Then he massaged it, turning it slowly until I felt better."

"Wafula, *daktari!*" Mama Angineta shouted.

"I told the man to let me go. He said, 'You're a fool. Where do you want to go at this time of night?'," Zuri said. "When I cried and said I wanted to go to my mother, the man got angry and told me to go."

"Finally! You were free," Penny said, jumping up and down.

"I walked out of the shack and walked away, but before long, I knew I was lost," Zuri said, biting her lower lip. "I could see the lights from the road, but then when I tried to get to them, I found myself walking in circles. I was about to sit down and cry when I looked behind me and saw the large man not far from where I was."

"Ohh no…make him go away, make him go away…" Penny said, her hands covering her face.

"Shut up, Penny," Kefa and Jimmo said once again.

"I forgot my injured foot and ran," Zuri continued. "I could not run far, though. The man grabbed me once again and slung me over his shoulder. I tried to fight him, kicking him and beating him with my fists, but he walked on through the bushes until he came to the road.

'You are now on Prof. Wangari Maathai Road, now walk and don't look back,' The man told me.

"I ran, crossing the road and almost getting knocked down by an oncoming vehicle. Then I walked to Thika Road, turning to Park Road and then past Pangani Police Station. The streets were deserted, but I knew I was not alone. I could sense him behind me. I got to Chai Road and boarded a vehicle to Estleigh, where I live with my mum. The man too got into the vehicle, and when the conductor came to ask for fare, the man paid for me."

"An angel of guardian," Penny said.

"A guardian angel Penny," Mr. Odhiambo said, laughing.

"I turned and stared at the man then. The man had a big head with hair sprinkled with gray. His neck was thick, and his shoulders were like those of the wrestlers we see on TV. His large hands rested on his thighs. His face was very dark, like a starless night. As dark as yours, Kefa," Zuri said.

"Where is he? Where is this man then?" Kefa asked, rising to his feet.

"The man followed me when I got out of the matatu and walked behind me to our estate. I knocked at our gate, and when the watchman opened, I turned to look back at the man, but he had disappeared.

# CHAPTER 12

Kefa sat down on the floor and put his head between his knees, feeling an ache in every part of his body. *The man had disappeared.* Zuri's words ran around in his head.

"So why did you come here tonight, Zuri? To see where I live and laugh at me?" Kefa asked.

"I came here because I wanted to help you," Zuri said.

"You don't even know where the man you claim is my father is," Kefa said.

Then, he walked out of the house. Zuri rose and followed him outside, and Kefa turned and pushed her back inside the house.

"Don't come near me. *Unaskia?*" Kefa told Zuri. "Go home to your parents and leave us alone."

"I only have my mother. I don't have a father," Zuri told him. "I have never seen him. He ran off before I was born."

"There was a man you were waving at, the Serena Hotel. He was not your father?" Kefa asked.

"That was him, Kefa. That was Mr. Wafula, your father," Zuri said.

"You are lying. I don't want to hear your lies anymore," Kefa said.

It was Mr. Odhiambo who brought Kefa back to the house.

"I went searching for your father, and I found him, Kefa," Zuri told Kefa.

"Do you remember when I was featured in the media having a rescued a street child from a gunfight?"

"What has that got to do with my father?" Kefa asked.

"I went back to City Park Kefa, to look for the man who had rescued me," Zuri said.

"I had been looking for him for a long time and that afternoon, I had decided I would not search anymore. I was about to cross one section of the park to go to another when I heard what sounded like a very loud tire burst, and I stood to listen. This was followed by a series of loud noises, sounding very close. I was about to step on to a path on the park when I saw the glint of metal. Someone was hiding behind the bush a few meters from where I was standing. Paralysed with fear, I stood where I was. The gunman came out of the bush, firing his gun. There was an immediate answer from the left. I dropped to the ground and lay where I was as Mrs. Njoroge, the Deputy Principal, had taught us once."

Zuri paused, and Kefa could see goose bumps covering her arms. "I could hear bullets flying all around me. The gun battle lasted for a few seconds. Then all was quiet but I lay where I was, afraid to move. Then when about five minutes had passed, I rose slowly. A second later, I dropped again to the ground. It had been a temporary lull. The gun battle resumed and this time, I closed my eyes and silently said my last prayers. When I opened my eyes, I saw something that shocked me. A child, of about two years, was walking unsteadily right on the path of flying bullets.

I acted purely out of instinct then although everyone later thought I was a hero," Zuri paused.

"You are a hero, a celeb!" Penny said.

"I don't think so, Penny. It was as if someone was directing my actions. I had risen from my hiding place and grabbed the child, dragging her to the bushes as bullets whistled past.

I learnt later that while I was walking into City Park, three thugs were robbing an M-Pesa agent along Limuru Road at gunpoint. Fortunately for the agent, there were two police officers patrolling the street and as they spotted the three men gang, they gave chase. The gang had run towards City Park with the police officers following.

At the end of the gunfight two thugs lay dead while one had escaped. One police officer had been shot in the shoulder. The child had not suffered even a scratch.

"You acted with courage, Zuri," Mr. Odhiambo told her.

"Oh, Mr. Odhiambo, I fainted when it all over," Zuri's said. "When I was coming to, I heard someone saying, 'Give her space, stand back.' I could see a large figure bending over me.

'Put something under her feet.' The man ordered the women standing by as he loosened my clothing. The man took a *Kikoi* from a woman who was standing nearby and covered me with it. I soon felt my strength returning and struggled to raise myself from the ground.

'Stay where you are for now and rest. You will be alright,' The man told me.

It was the same man who had rescued me from the thugs. The man I believe is your father, Kefa.

"After I had rested and people had dispersed, he took me inside his shack at the park."

"Let's go then. Right now!" Kefa said.

"We won't find the shack in the dark. It is so well concealed behind a bush that one can pass right by even during the day and not see it," Zuri said.

"We can use torches. I need to see this man tonight," Kefa said, "Mama, call Mama Nasimiyu to come and pick Naliaka."

"We can't go to City Park at night, Kefa, it could be dangerous. We have to wait until morning," the Principal said.

"Actually, we don't have to go to the park," Zuri said. "Baba Wafula, that is what we call him, comes to my mother's *kibanda* every day to bring her groceries from Marikiti."

"You are sure about this?" Mr. Odhiambo asked.

"Yes," Zuri said, then she chuckled.

"What is very funny that you're laughing?" Penny asked.

"What's so funny, Penny," Zuri said. "Anyway, after I had met Baba Wafula, I kept going back to the park to take him food. That is why I gave that scarf you were asking me about Penny,  to a street girl in the park. Every time I took him food, he would call a few street children and share the food with them. One day one of the children was shivering from cold and I gave her my scarf."

"You should have given it to me," Penny said, pouting.

"Don't be so selfish. As I was saying, my mother has a grocery store in Ngara, and for a long time, she has been sharing the space with Mr. Njuguna, who had a *mitura* stand. Then Mr. Njuguna died, and his sons have been running their father's business. They could not raise the monthly rent, and my mother allowed them to continue when they promised they would pay soon. It has now been three months, and Mama has been paying the county council rates alone. A few days ago, Mama told them they had to pay rent or take their Mutura *jiko* elsewhere. The following day, Mama and I found Njuguna's sons had built a shed behind the store. Mama tried to tell them it was not allowed by the Nairobi County Council, but they threatened to beat her up. Then they started throwing garbage at the door of my mother's store.

One Saturday, when Mama had gone to the Marikiti market and left me in charge, one of Mr. Njuguna's sons, Muya, walked to the grocery store and selected a few of the best tomatoes, *dhania*, and onions and walked away without paying. I tried to get the money from them, and one of them twisted my hand behind my back. I told my mother when she came back and when she went to confront them, they wanted to attack her. She was only saved by some mechanics who work nearby. The boys thought they were clever. *Lakini!*"

"You beat them? Karate hwa, hwa," Penny said, slicing the air with her hands.

"No. I don't know any karate, Penny. I went to City Park and told Baba Wafula. The following day, being a Sunday, Njuguna's sons did not open their mitura place until after ten. Mama and I stood at the balcony of a nearby house, waiting and watching. Mwihuri was the first to arrive, and I saw him standing gaping at the empty place where their shed had stood. It had been dismantled, and the old iron sheets and wood they had used to build it were laid neatly in a pile. Next to the pile was their jiko. Muya, his younger brother, joined him soon after.

Both men rushed to Mama's grocery store. The next moment Baba Wafula came out holding the two men by their belts like the police usually do, their feet not touching the ground, and then he threw them outside. Weru, the youngest, who had just arrived to find his brothers being dragged out of the grocery store, stood open-mouthed staring at Baba Wafula."

"*Mtoto wa Enjofu kabisa,*" Mama Angineta said that Wafula was indeed Enjofu's son.

"From that day on, my mother asked him to be carrying our groceries from Marikiti to her store.'

"If this man looks like me, how come you never said anything until now?" Kefa asked Zuri.

"I never thought he could be your father because I knew very little about you, but now *niko* sure. He is the one."

"We won't know until we meet the man," Mr. Odhiambo told Kefa. "We have to wait until morning, though. It's late, and we need to get back."

"But I want to see him now," Kefa said, his voice thick with emotion.

Kefa's relief at hearing his father had been found was quickly replaced with overwhelming anger. He wanted his father to answer the questions that had disturbed him for almost three years. Mr. Odhiambo rose and put his arm around Kefa's shoulders.

"Be a little patient. Tomorrow we will go and find your father."

# CHAPTER 13

Kefa, his mother, three brothers, his three classmates, and Mr. Odhiambo, waited at the grocery store run by Wanjiru, Zuri's mother. The Principal, Kefa's family, Jimmo and Penny had come very early and found Zuri and her mother already at the grocery store. Wanjiru had told them, "Wafula usually brings groceries by seven o'clock." However, seven o'clock came and passed, but there was no sign of Wafula. At eight o'clock, Wanjiru said, "I am going to the Marikiti market to look for him." Kefa could hardly sit still. So restless was he. Kefa's younger brothers, Simiyu and Situma, had been called from St. Martins rehabilitation centre and they too waited eagerly for their father.

"It's not him," Kefa, who was the first to spot Wanjiru and the man who was carrying her groceries approaching, said.

Kefa saw the brown, short, and stocky man and turned accusing eyes at Zuri.

"That is not my father. You lied to us."

The previous night Kefa had finally been convinced that the man Zuri was talking about could be his long-lost father after she had described the tall big man she knew as Wafula. Kefa had hardly slept and had lain awake anxiously waiting for daybreak. He wanted to confront the man who had abandoned them. The man who had made his mother age before her time, with worry lines edged deep in on her face. He wanted the man to answer for making him and his brothers into street boys who searched dumpsites like scavengers looking for scraps to eat.

His father's absence had affected all of them deeply. Juma had withdrawn into himself and hardly spoke unless spoken to. Simiyu and Situma had lost their playfulness, the harsh realities of life having been thrust upon them too early. Naliaka, who had been a toddler when her father disappeared, kept asking her mother, "Why don't I have a father like other children?" Then there was Mama Angineta's look of emptiness as if she had lost the spark of life. She seemed to be waiting and waiting. Kefa did not want to imagine what this new disappointment could do to her.

"He is not the man I was talking about. Wafula does not look like that," Zuri said, shaking her head, her eyes shining with unshed tears.

"Wafula was not at the market," Wanjiru said, sitting down wearily. "Some people at the market told me there was an accident at the market early in the morning. A sack of potatoes fell on someone's foot. I don't know if it was Wafula, and no one seemed to know. I looked for him all over the market, and I couldn't find him."

"He has disappeared once again. He must have known we were looking for him and ran off," Kefa said. "I hate him!"

"Don't say that, Kefa," his mother said, putting her hand on her mouth. Kefa kept quiet, knowing the waiting to see Wafula was as hard for Mama Angineta as it was for him.

The group at Wanjiru's grocery store waited for an hour then decided to go to City Park. Zuri led the way to Wafula's shack. In less than twenty-four hours, burial rites would be performed in Bungoma. Then Kefa knew the family would truly become destitute. *Where is my father, and why can't we find him?* Kefa asked himself.

They went to the shack that Zuri had spoken of, but when they thrust the door open, they found the shack empty. Upon revealing the empty room, Kefa hit his fist against his palm. Tears fell silently from Mama Angineta's eyes. She looked around Wafula's humble dwelling, touching his things. A few utensils were stacked inside a plastic bucket. There was a mattress on the floor with a worn blanket rolled on top. A pair of plastic slippers were near the door, with one slipper in front of the other as if whoever had won them had removed them in a hurry.

"He can't have gone far," Mr. Odhimbo said. "His things are still here."

"Where is he then? Where is he?" Kefa asked.

It was Situma who was the first to see his father. He came out of the shack for some air. As he stepped out, Situma came face to face with his father.

"Baba!" Situma's cry brought everyone from inside the shack.

Were it not for Mr. Odhiambo, Kefa would have rushed at his father with fists. Mr. Odhiambo grabbed Kefa before he could hit his father. So great was his anger.  Kefa wanted to hit the man who had caused him and his family so much misery. Kefa struggled to free himself, but Mr. Odhiambo held fast.

"Why, Baba, why?" Kefa asked his father.

Zuri and Penny broke down in tears.

Wafula stood as if paralyzed. Only his eyes moved from one member of his family to the next. Then his eyes rested on Kefa's mother, Angineta. She did not say a word, but her eyes were wet with tears. Then something seemed to come over him, and he started shaking. Mr. Odhiambo had to let go of Kefa, and both he and Mama Angineta rushed to Wafula and held the big man as his legs gave, and they gently lowered him to the ground.

Mr. Odhiambo, Zuri, Penny, and Jimmo traveled that evening to Kimilili, Bungoma. They were taking Wafula and his family home. They traveled in the Mugumo Primary School van. Kefa's parents sat in front talking, and his father told his mother everything.

"I lost my job, and that's when I suffered a nervous breakdown. This morning, I was injured by a sack of potatoes falling from a lorry and had had to go to a dispensary at the city centre."

Kefa listened in. Kefa's three friends Zuri, Jimmo, and Penny, sat with little Naliaka and kept her entertained. Kefa and Mr. Odhiambo sat at the back. Kefa had refused to talk to his father.

When his father had recovered from the shock, it was his mother who had explained the situation at home.

"I will never forgive my father," Kefa muttered, under his breath.

"You heard the man Kefa, he could not bear to come home when he lost his job," Mr. Odhiambo told him.

"You don't understand sir. It has been so hard for us. My mother does *kibarua*, casual jobs just to feed us. I almost got killed in the streets."

"Your father has been a street person for more than three years now. It must have been very difficult for him too."

"It wasn't fair to do this to us. *Sio poa*," Kefa said.

"Life is not always fair, Kefa, and you are wrong. I do understand. You see, I was not always Mr. Odhiambo, the Principal, that you see. My mother struggled to raise us just like yours. My father abandoned us and went to live with another woman not far from where we lived. Can you imagine how hard it was to watch the woman's children well-dressed and well-fed when we had nothing to eat?"

Kefa shook his head, his face gloomy. He, too, was thinking about the pain of an empty stomach.

"When I was in standard eight, my mother was unable to raise the money to register for the final exam," Mr. Odhiambo continued. "As the deadline drew near, I became desperate and went to my father for help. I found him with the woman he had moved in with, and when I asked him for the money, he told me, 'I do not have it.'

The woman turned to me and said, 'Why are you bothering to register? Even if you pass the exam, your mother won't afford to pay for your secondary school education, and your father here won't pay for you.'

I looked at my father, and he remained silent, and I turned and left.

As I walked away, I heard the woman say, 'I hear he is always the top pupil at Rabiki Primary School. What a waste.'

Then she laughed. You can imagine how I felt towards my father then.

My mother sold the only thing with some value that my father had left us with, a fourteen-inch black and white television. She paid the registration fee, but even as I studied for the exam, I felt hopeless. I had a friend I used to compete with in-class called Karis, and he told me that in their mother tongue they have a saying that, '*Mwana wi kiyo ndagaga muthambia*,' which loosely translated means, 'A hardworking child will not fail to get someone to help him or her.' Well, I worked hard and passed my exams, and sure enough, a charitable foundation paid for my secondary school education."

"Did you finally forgive your father?" Kefa asked.

"Not for a long time," Mr. Odhiambo responded.

Then asked, "Do you know Belinda Achieng in standard eight?"

Kefa nodded.

"That is my stepsister, and she stays at my house while attending school. My father died a few years ago, and his second wife followed soon after. Their four children were left with no one to look after them. I wanted nothing to do with them as I was still angry at my father. It was my mother who talked some sense into me. She told me, 'If you do not help your stepbrothers and sisters, you will be just as bad as your father.' She actually told me I would be worse - because I knew better."

"It won't be easy to forgive him, Mr. Odhiambo," Kefa said thoughtfully. "My father left me when I needed him most."

Kefa, as a young child, had viewed his father almost with awe. To the young boy, he was superman. He was the cleverest man who knew what to do in every situation. Villagers could come when Wafula was at home to ask for advice on minor ailments.

Kefa had watched his father splitting huge logs of wood with great strength and helping a calving cow with utmost gentleness. When his father disappeared, Kefa had lost the person he most looked up to, and it had made feel lost too like a person in a maze without a guide. Now everything was beginning to feel clear again as if he had finally found his way again.

The group taking Kefa's father home from Nairobi traveled all night, and they made it to Sikhedu village in Kimilili at around ten o'clock in the morning. The van stopped a few meters from the

Wafula's homestead, and Kefa and Zuri got out and walked into the compound. Kefa could see that his uncle had not spared any expense. Meat was roasting in pits while more was being cooked in large *sufurias*. Young, energetic men were turning moulds of ugali.

"This looks more like a feast than burial rites," Zuri said.

"My uncle is celebrating now, but shock on him, his celebration will soon come to an end," Kefa said.

People stopped what they were doing and stared at the two as they made their way into the homestead. Kefa asked someone where Sitati, his uncle, was and was directed to a small hut. Uncle Sitati was sitting at the far end of the room with a group of men. He was smartly dressed in a new navy-blue suit. There were several guards of *Busaa*, and the men were busy taking the brew.

"You don't have to come all the way here, Waswa," Musinai, a friend of Uncle Sitati who was seated next to him, was telling a man whom Kefa recognized as Waswa, their neighbor on the northern side. Waswa had passed them on the road as they were getting off the school van.

"I am sure the son of Wanyonyi can order another gourd to be brought," Musinai added.

"Actually, Waswa should not sit far from the entrance," Uncle Sitati said with a chuckle then, turning to a man who was nearby, explained. "You see, Waswa has one wife. A man who has one wife has to sit where he can get up quickly and leave. If a messenger comes and tells me that something has happened to my wife, I will have time to move from where I am sitting while enquiring about which wife. However, a man with one wife will not have the time!"

"As a matter of fact, I think you are the one who needs to leave the room now," Waswa told Uncle Sitati, pointing at the door where Kefa and Zuri stood.

"We have been sent to ask you to come with us," Kefa told his uncle after he and Zuri had exchanged greetings with everyone around.

"Who has sent you?" Uncle Sitati asked. "If it is your mother, go back and tell her to come and join everyone. This is her home she should not fear to come right in."

"There is someone else who wants to see you," Kefa said. "You should come with a few elders."

The men in the room rose and walked outside the compound with Uncle Sitati following. Uncle Sitati's eldest wife and several women followed the men, and a sizable crowd stopped near the Mugumo Primary School van. Jimmo and Penny, who was holding Naliaka by the hand, disembarked from the van followed by Juma, Simiyu, and Situma. Curious onlookers edged closer to the van. Mr. Odhiambo got off the van too.

"Didn't you say all Wafula's children were adopted?" Waswa asked Uncle Sitati.

"That is what I was told. That their mother sold them," Uncle Sitati said.

Then Mama Angineta disembarked.

"It's Mama Angineta!" a woman sad.

"She has come back!" another one said.

"Welcome home, *mulamwa*," Sitati said, extending his hand. "It is good to see my late brother's wife back home, where she belongs."

"Thanks, Mulamwa. I have come back for good," Mama Angineta said, her voice as soft as the gentle wind. Her eyes looked straight into Sitati's.

The door of the van had slid shut when Mama Angineta was getting off. The driver got off the vehicle and came around to open it. Wafula stepped out.

Those close to the van turned and fled, running into those behind them. The women rent the air with their screams. Sitati was knocked down in the melee, and as he struggled from the ground, he looked up to the tall figure of his brother Wafula. There was a chill in the morning air, but beads of sweat formed on Uncle Sitati's forehead.

"It's an abomination for one brother to wish another dead," Wafula told Uncle Sitati.

"I n... Never wished you dead, my brother. I was told you had died and been buried in Nairobi," Sitati responded.

"Then I am back from the dead, and I am not going to leave my family ever again," Wafula said.

"Do you really mean that, Baba?" Kefa asked his father.

"Yes, Kefa. I am going to work hard and look after all of you. I should not have stayed away. I know that now."

"You should not have stayed away," Kefa said.

"I wanted to come back, many times but I would ask myself, *What do I have to offer my family when I don't have a job?"* Wafula said.

"Oh Baba, you are our father, the head of our family. My brothers and sister needed you, and Mama, she had missed you so. We are so happy to have you back with us," Kefa said.

"It is like the return of the prodigal son," Penny said.

"I don't quite see the connection Penny, but my father is home, thanks to you all," Kefa told his friends and for the first in many weeks, he smiled, a big smile that stretched from ear to ear, showing strong white teeth, like those of his father.

"Are you going to go back to Nairobi Kefa?" Zuri asked.

"My brothers might stay here with my parents, but I will go back. I will stay with Mr. Odhiambo and complete my primary education at Mugumo Primary School," Kefa said.

"Perhaps the four of us can start another project for street children," Zuri said.

"I would like that," Kefa said.